# A Horse in New York

*Other Avon Camelot Books by*
**Cam Parker**

CAMP OFF-THE-WALL

# A Horse in New York

## Cam Parker

AN AVON CAMELOT BOOK

AVON BOOKS
A division of
The Hearst Corporation
105 Madison Avenue
New York, New York 10016

To the Ace of Hearts—Entrepreneur

# Chapter One

"Tiffin Roswel" the envelope read. My last name was spelled wrong, it has two *l*'s, but at least the letter was addressed to me. I was happy to see it. I like finding mail after school. I said hello to our dog, Fluff, dropped the rest of the mail and my book bag onto the kitchen table, and prepared to read my letter. It was from Mr. Hildebrande, the owner of the camp I went to last summer, Chucalucup, on the banks of Lake Noswminaloud—at least that's what a sign near the water proclaimed.

Why was Mr. Hildebrande writing to me? I wondered as I opened the envelope quickly. Could it be a forgotten bill from his fast food and take out tent? Maybe it was the special offer of a ten percent discount on the price of camp next summer—if my parents would pay for next summer now. But I'd heard that would come in a holiday greeting card. That was months away. This turned out to be a real letter, a serious letter about my camp horse, Blue. He needed a home, and I needed to help him find one. Unfortunately for both of

1

us, the letter came the same day Daddy moved out of our apartment for the second time this year. That made it very difficult to help Blue with his problems; my parents were too busy having problems of their own.

They were separating again and weren't going into the reasons, but one of the reasons had recently occurred at a rock concert my father escorted me and my friend Tara to. Tara wanted to see the U-Hauls; they're her favorite group and this was their first concert in New York. I just wanted to see a rock concert, any rock concert. It would be my first anywhere.

What happened there wasn't exactly my father's fault. He wasn't even supposed to chaperone us in the first place. Mama was supposed to. She'd agreed to it one night when she came home from her law office very late and full of guilt for not spending more time with my younger brother, Wil, and me. She even ordered the tickets. But at the last minute, she had to attend an important meeting. Mama wants to be a judge. Our family friend Arthur recommended her to an honesty-in-government citizens group, which didn't want to endorse a candidate they hadn't met. The group was meeting that night, so the concert was out, unless my father took us.

"You're just trying to transfer your guilt to me," my father told her in the patient tone of voice he uses in his office. He's a psychologist.

"And you're being very uncooperative," my mother responded in her reasonable courtroom manner. She said that the tickets were already charged and would go to waste at the box office if he didn't take us. That argument was immensely appealing to my father. As far as he's concerned the idea of spending money is bad enough. The idea of wasting it is almost intolerable.

"The tickets are already charged?" he asked, looking stunned.

"Yes. All you have to do is show them the credit card at the box office. If the cabfare is bothering you, consider it my treat."

"I am not being a cheapskate," my father said nasally. "And if I do go, I'm taking the car."

Mama again suggested we take a cab. But my father insisted on taking the car. My mother shuddered. She refers to our car as the movable heap. Recently she tried to make a bargain with my father that if he would pay for a new car, she would pay for a garage. He refused. He said they don't make cars like his anymore. "Beside which," he'd added, "it's paid for."

"A cab is out of the question," my father said. "We'd have a hard time finding one now, and it would be impossible after the concert. There's a parking garage directly across the street," he added. "We can zip right in, park, and cross the street to pick up the tickets." He quietly reckoned that one parking lot would cost less than taxis to and from the concert. "It's all settled," he said.

Unfortunately, no one had told the parking attendant it was all settled. The garage was full when we got there. Daddy couldn't believe his ears.

3

"Full?" he asked the parking attendant, who kept shouting, "Back it up," in our direction.

"What do you mean, full?" my father asked when the man paused to take a breath.

"I mean there's no more room for cars," he explained patiently. "Back it up. Back it up."

"But we're going right across the street," my father protested. "What am I going to do with my car?"

"I don't know, sir," he said and smiled, "but you can't do it here; back it up, back it up."

"Don't worry, girls," my father said. "There are three other garages around here."

We drove around the block six times, because the three other garages were full too.

"Don't worry, girls," my father said coolly, but with a dry rasp in his voice. "Everything is under control."

"Daddy," I said, as another empty cab drove by, "we could have been there by now. We're going to be late."

"I'm taking care of it," he said, looking desperately out the windshield. "I'm taking care of it."

The traffic came to a temporary stop, and Daddy leaned out his window to speak to a mounted policeman. I spoke to his horse while he told my father the only thing to do was park at a lot eight blocks away and take a taxi back.

"Daddy," I said, after Tara poked me with her elbow, "we're late already."

"I know," he said. "I know. But I'm taking care of it. Say," he asked suddenly as the traffic began to move, "did he say we should make a left at the corner or go straight ahead?"

Daddy made a left turn and managed to go around the block again as we begged him to drive us to the box office entrance.

"Pulleeze," we both said with our hands clasped together, "Pulleeze." He finally agreed. Then he made a long speech about strange characters in this world, and who not to talk to at the concert—everybody in the world. Then he said something about not going to the toilets alone. Then he gave us his wallet containing his credit cards, because he wasn't sure which account my mother had used, and said he'd meet us in the parents' quiet room after the concert.

He remained in front of the concert hall and watched us rush up to the box office for our tickets and rush inside. Then he drove across town to park. He intended to take one of the very many empty cabs right back, until he remembered to his horror that he'd given me his wallet. At least he remembered before he hailed a taxi. He walked as fast as he could for the first four blocks. Then he jogged for the next three, even though he wasn't wearing jogging shoes. He jogged till he got two blisters, one on each heel, and the only way he could walk without pain was in a stiff-kneed Frankenstein kind of way. Then, one of his shoelaces broke and he groped his way along the buildings of the last block dragging that foot. He was out of breath as he climbed the few steps to the box office, one straight leg at a time. He had to hold out his arms a little to keep his balance,

5

because he didn't usually walk that way. The people in the box office thought he was coming to eat them.

He leaned against the ticket booth gasping for air and soaked with perspiration. Then he peered through the little barred window, as his hair settled down damply onto his forehead.

Daddy explained the situation between gulps of air and grunts of pain, as he shifted from one wounded heel the other. He told them quickly that we were supposed to meet at the parents' quiet room after the concert, "also before and after going to the toilet," he added urgently. He promised to pay for his ticket then. He was still catching his breath, so he rested his head on the brass bars of the box office window just as a drop of perspiration slid around the corner of his mouth and slowly down the side of his chin. The people in the box office pressed themselves to the opposite wall.

Just then a charter bus came to a quick stop at the curb. Its doors opened, and a horde of senior citizens hurried off. It was the Goldy Oldys, a group that attends rock concerts to keep active. They hurried their way up the stairs and through the lobby. They crowded past Daddy, and as they did he clunked along, side to side through the entrance doors.

Once inside, he began looking for us, while the security guards began looking for him. Daddy clunked upstairs and downstairs in his peculiar walk, and they charged upstairs and downstairs after him. They appeared on every balcony. First

**6**

Daddy would stomp quickly onto the scene like the monster returned. He'd look for us and stomp quickly out again. The guards would then do the same thing, except they were looking for him. The audience began to notice the chase, and some of them began to cheer him on. Then all of them began to cheer him on. I did too, but it was dark in the theater and it never occurred to me that it was my father.

A camera crew began to tape the chase as the U-Hauls began their new hit song, "I Can Hear a Pin Drop." We could hardly hear them because the guards were shouting "There he goes, there he goes." Daddy suddenly appeared at the side of the stage and stomped stiffly down the stairs and into the seats. His shoe came off, and when he stopped to retrieve it, he was surrounded. He picked up his shoe and climbed on a seat, and he was carried out calling my name.

"Tiffin," Tara asked me. "Did I just hear what I think I heard?"

"I certainly hope not," I said.

They rushed Dad outside, and he had to explain everything to a policeman as he held his shoe and wiped his forehead with the Day-Glo bandana I gave him for his birthday. I bought it on sale last summer at Mr. Hildebrande's boutique and credit candy store. It says ELVIS LIVES on both sides. My father carries it to make up for the strange face he made the day I gave it to him. "Just come along quietly," the policeman said gently. "I'll take you to see Elvis."

That night, Mama's first act as the honest-government candidate was to bail my father out of jail.

"Well, you didn't have to stand on a seat!" Mama said, after she'd pleaded his case in night court. She'd had to leave her meeting, pick up Tara and me, take us home, then go represent Daddy.

"Everyone was standing on a seat," my father said calmly.

"That's no excuse," Mama said. "And please put your shoes on!"

Mama won a dismissal by presenting it as temporary parental insanity. The judge had children too and said he understood how it is sometimes. "You're lucky the magistrate thought it was only temporary," Mama said slowly. "Do you know how embarrassing this was for me? Can you imagine?"

"I don't wish to discuss it," Daddy said, with his voice very high in his throat.

Things began to get very polite around the house in the days that followed. That convinced me that Wil and I would be making a lot of dinners for ourselves soon.

Usually, when my parents aren't in one of their moods—that is, when they're being nice to each other instead of just polite—they take turns on who comes home from whose office first to put something into the microwave. Then we gather round the dinner table while Dad opens the plastic pouches that steam-fry his fingers. It's one of his chores. In exchange, my mother puts the reusable trays into the dishwasher and throws them away

**8**

when they come out warped. It's a very satisfactory arrangement, and we get a chance to discuss things over very hot food.

However, after the concert, my parents began to see who could arrive home after the other had popped dinner into the oven. Mama devoted more time to her political career, and Daddy gave one of his patients an evening appointment.

I had to zap dinner for my brother Wil and me four nights in a row. That wasn't a good sign.

Then on Thursday I received the letter from camp about Blue. I sat very quietly for a long time after I read it. Blue needed my help. It sounded very much like a matter of life and death. I wanted to discuss Blue's problem around the dinner table that night, but it didn't look as if that was going to happen, under the circumstances.

Actually, they both came home from work early that evening and announced that we were going out to dinner. Wil and I knew they were going to gently break the news that they weren't getting along again. It wasn't exactly a surprise. At least this time it wouldn't feel so much like the end of the world. Their choice of restaurants for the occasion was a place that arranges the food into pictures on the plates. My parents get formal at times like these. We'd been there before. It was last spring, on the evening of their first separation. We even had the same waiter. His name is Woodie, and he's really a drama student, and he remembered us as "those nice polite people."

Wil ordered chopped steak, which came in the form of a sunflower, with the burger as its center, and french fries as petals. It looked very nice; I was sorry I hadn't ordered it. My sliced chicken came fashioned as a hen with a string-bean nest of tiny potato eggs. I wondered which part of my dinner I could eat with a clear conscience. I didn't bother to look at my parents' plates, and they didn't seem to either.

Just about all I could think of was Blue, but somehow it just wasn't the right night to raise more problems for my parents. Even the barnyard scene on my plate reminded me of Blue's predicament. In fact, everything reminded me of it. The letter from Mr. Hildebrande said that Blue needed a place to live until summer, and I was his last winter resort.

Mr. Hildebrande had managed to place all the other horses for the winter, mostly with campers who lived in the suburbs or the country. Only my horse Blue was left. He's a little unusual and hard to find a home for, and I live in the middle of the city.

I popped a potato egg in my mouth and blurted that I had a giant, important, life or death problem. Usually that gets my parents' attention, but no one was really listening. I repeated it a little more loudly as I cut off my hen's head and shuddered; but my parents were busy being very polite to each other, and my brother Wil was busy mapping soccer plays on his napkin.

Mama did pay attention long enough to tell me never to speak with a potato in my mouth. Then she and my father went back to making civilized chitchat.

"The leaves changed color very early this year," one of them said.

"Yes, they did," the other agreed.

"Would you please pass the rolls?"

"Of course."

"Are they warm?"

"Yes."

"That always makes such a difference."

"Yes, it does. Here's a nice one."

"Thank you."

"You're welcome."

It wasn't the moment to tell my parents that I desperately needed to keep a horse in the city this winter. I carefully reattached the head of my chicken.

Then Daddy told Wil and me that he and Mama had something to say to us, and would Wil please stop drawing on the tablecloth. He'd already used both sides of his napkin and was now making his way around the plates. Woodie came to the table and smiled tensely at Wil. Then he looked at my chicken. "You didn't eat much at all," he said in a disappointed voice that managed to attract both my parents' at once.

"I'm saving room for dessert," I announced quickly. I knew he'd be pleased. Restaurants always are when you order dessert. Woodie left for a moment, and returned just as my parents announced that they were having problems. He looked startled, but gave me my dessert. It was three colors of sugar-free sherbet molded in the shape of a honeybee. I felt like an absolute fiend eating it.

11

Woodie disappeared and returned with coffee just as my parents stated that they weren't getting along. That came as another big surprise to him. He'd just said they were very polite, and we were the perfect family. I could see him register shock and disbelief on his face at the news. I think that was his dramatic training.

Woodie spilled some coffee and took a long time wiping it up while Daddy said they just needed some time away from each other to think things over.

Woodie looked at Mama and held his breath. Then Daddy said they weren't going to go into any details. This was strictly between them. Woodie looked very disappointed and exhaled. No one spoke for a few minutes, so he shrugged his shoulders sadly and left.

Then one of my parents mentioned something about my mother's decision to run for a judgeship, and Daddy's lack of enthusiasm for it.

Then someone said the other wasn't interested in anyone's career but his own, and how he never spent quality time with anybody anymore. Then they became even more very polite to each other.

"Would you care for more coffee?"

"No, thank you."

"You're welcome."

It was very quiet while we waited for the check. I started to bring up the matter of Blue again. Actually, I started to clear my throat in order to start to bring up the matter of Blue, but Daddy began saying he'd always be there to help me with my algebra, which wasn't wonderful news to me. It's not that I don't appreciate my father's interest in my math homework, but he always starts by saying, "That's not the way we did it when I was a kid."

Then he explains how to do the problem the way he used to do it. It always sounds something like, "Count to ten, add backwards, and subtract three, except when you have to multiply by five because dividing by seventeen doesn't work. You see, it's simple."

After Dad was finished promising me eternal interest in my studies, he turned his attention to Wil. He promised Wil he'd always be there to kick a soccer ball with. That came as a surprise. The last time my father kicked a soccer ball, it bounced off his foot and into a tree, and bounced off the tree and onto his nose. He had to lie down for an hour.

After Dad was done reassuring Wil of a playmate, he reached across the restaurant table and squeezed my arm. Then he squeezed Wil's arm. Woodie saw us from across the room and dabbed one eye with a napkin.

Mama said she and Daddy were still the best of friends.

"Thank you," he said.

"You're welcome," she answered.

Woodie brought us the check, and when we were leaving, he hugged Mom. "Keep in touch," he said. Then he shook hands with Dad, "I'm always here," he told him. Then he saw us to the door and dabbed his other eye with his sleeve.

We went back to our apartment, and Daddy

packed a suitcase. At least he wouldn't have to carry it on an empty stomach. He said he'd be at the university club until he could make other arrangements. Wil and I took that to mean until he moved back home again.

After Daddy left, our dog, Fluff, sat listening for his footsteps in the hall. They have a special relationship. She was waiting to sink her teeth into parts of his feet again. It helps her relax between meals.

# Chapter Two

Fluff was still waiting by the door the next morning. She cocked her head from side to side, growling hopefully at every sound that passed in the hall. I waved her very favorite rubber bone in her face to try to take her mind off her troubles, but she didn't even bother to sniff it.

My brother, Wil, held one of my father's shoes under her nose, and Fluff looked at it for a few seconds. Since my father's foot was nowhere in sight, she lost interest in it and us, until we gave her something to eat.

Mama was very quiet during breakfast. I wanted to talk about Blue, but instead I asked her if the neighbors who talk about us on the elevator, talk about us in their apartments too.

"What makes you think they're talking about us at all?" she asked, checking her briefcase, which was sitting on Dad's empty chair at the table. Mom wanted to make sure she hadn't forgotten to pack anything important. She likes to keep her briefcase nearby at all times, so if there's an earthquake or something, she can check to see that all her papers are in order. Usually, it rests on the floor next to her feet, but since there was an empty place at the table, it joined us for breakfast.

"The last time this happened, with Dad I mean, I had the unfortunate experience of riding up on the elevator with Mr. and Mrs. Clyme from next door," I said, swirling melted butter into my oatmeal with the tip of my spoon. "He was coming from the supermarket pulling a shopping cart full of groceries, and she was coming from the laundry room pushing a supermarket cart full of clothes."

I'd just come back from a riding lesson in Central Park and was carrying my saddle. I was willing to wait until they finished with the elevator, but they said there was plenty of room, so I got on. Well, between his cart, her cart, and my saddle, we did a kind of square dance for the first two floors.

Then somehow his cart got squeezed into the wall behind Mrs. Clyme and me, and everything went totally silent as we listened to a dozen eggs crack. The Clymes looked at each other very very intensely for a while.

Then they looked at their groceries intensely for a while, and so did I, as a large wet spot began to form at the bottom of one of the bags. They weren't the only ones who had a reason to be upset. I certainly didn't feel like standing in raw eggs on the elevator. Then the Clymes looked very intensely at me.

16

"Mrs. Clyme pursed her lips and said something about broken homes, and smelling like horses." Which I think is a perfectly pleasing smell.

"Mr. Clyme said something about, 'an emergency meeting of the board, and smelling like horses.' I hugged my saddle as they eyed me like two hungry crows in a cornfield.

"So I was wondering, Mom," I said, chewing on a spoonful of thick oatmeal, "do people who talk about other people, only talk about them on elevators, or do they go home and talk about them there too?"

"Tiffin, dear," my mother said in her most legal tone of voice—the one she saves for clients who pay late. "If talking about us is all our neighbors have to do, then they are in more trouble than we." I wondered what my mother meant by "more trouble than we." I didn't know we were in any trouble at all. I know that some people might call our family relationship troubled. I know that according to several television movies I was supposed to be on the verge of collapse, but I really didn't feel that way this time. My parents seemed to agree that one of the things that held their marriage together was their separations. Maybe they needed to call a time-out every once in a while just to catch their breaths.

Mom said I'd understand it better when I got older. That was something to look forward to. I once asked my grandmother what she thought of it all. Her opinion was that my parents were going through a difficult stage. When I asked her what the stage was, she said, "Life."

17

I was prepared to accept that. At least it was something I could be reasonably sure of. The other thing I could reasonably be sure of was that for the duration of their separation, Daddy would send us strange presents. My mother explained that my father's increased generosity at times like these was his way of dealing with his feelings of guilt about leaving. The last time they separated, he mail ordered Wil and me a crate of ruby red grapefruit from Texas. I guess he was feeling guilty about our getting enough vitamin C.

Then, just to show us all that he and Mama were still good friends, he mail ordered her a beautiful bunch of lifelike plastic roses. You could hardly tell they weren't real, unless you felt, smelled, or looked at them closely. Daddy once told us that discarding wilted flowers was basically depressing. He was right, in a way. Mama looked very cheerful about throwing the plastic ones directly into the garbage even before they gathered dust. She did save the note he sent with them though, and tucked it into her purse. That seemed like a friendly thing to do.

If anybody was in trouble now it was Blue. According to Mr. Hildebrande's letter, time was running out for poor Blue. Mr. Hildebrande runs a clam bar in Florida for the winter, and I suppose he was anxious to get there and start digging for clams.

I finished my breakfast while all the awful stories about horses and glue factories flashed into my mind. I think that was due to the consistency of my oatmeal.

I wasn't sure what Mom would think about making a home for a horse in the city just then. I wasn't even sure what she'd think of it in the best of times, although I had a pretty good idea. I'd mentioned it just before camp ended, and she said she wasn't ready to spend as much money on a horse's stall as some people pay for an apartment. My father was living at home then, and when he's living at home, he doesn't like to talk about spending money at all.

I knew that if I brought up Blue's problem in Mom's current mood, the outcome would be certain. She'd listen carefully but impatiently before passing judgment. I could almost hear a gavel bang someplace. "No!"

My mother finished her coffee, and she and I cleared the breakfast dishes while Wil—who thinks he's some kind of soccer god just because he's the star of his team and they've won every game— banged the dust from his knee pads into the air.

He'd spent most of breakfast looking for pieces of his soccer uniform. He dropped his team shirt into his duffel bag, and inspected the cleats on his soccer shoes for signs of yesterday's mud. Then he pushed his soccer shoes into his bag and onto his shirt.

"Mom," Wil asked, as we prepared to leave the apartment, my mother bound for her office, he and I to school. "Do you really want to be a judge?"

"Yes, I think I do," she said.

Before he left even my father finally promised to help.

He said he'd participate in any televised interviews with the candidate's family, if it was strictly necessary. He gave us a short talk on family ties, and all of us sticking together, and how he and Mom would always stick together. Then Fluff bit him on the ankle and he left.

My mother said she was touched, even though Dad insisted on the right to mention his office address and telephone number on television in return for his unselfish participation. He said it would be a public service announcement for any listeners who might need the services of a shrink.

"And that," Dad said to Mom, and smiled sweetly, "probably includes Arthur and the entire nominating committee."

"That," my mother smiled nicely and said, "probably includes you."

Mom, Wil, and I all left the apartment together that morning. That wasn't what we usually did, so just for the occasion, I wore a new dress my mother had surprised me with. The three of us had the elevator entirely to ourselves. Will stood near the door examining the seams of his soccer ball. Mama looked through her briefcase once more. I listened quietly for the sound of neighbors' voices talking about us. The only sound was Mama shuffling through her papers. Maybe everybody else was still asleep.

When we got to the lobby, our doorman Biff said a cheery good morning, and looked at us sympathetically. Mama responded by raising her chin and assuming her unstricken and brave expression.

Biff touched the brim of his hat in respect for my mother's courage in the face of a strange husband. Mama smiled bravely, and took in a deep brave breath through her nose. For a minute there, I half expected Biff to give her a light punch of encouragement on her arm. Instead he gave her a quick thumbs-up signal, which I thought was a little familiar, but we've known him a long time, and I guess he was trying to help. Biff opened the door and held it for us, and then followed our courageous band out of the building and onto the sidewalk.

It wasn't surprising that Biff already knew that Daddy had moved out. There aren't many secrets in a co-op. It's like a little village, and everybody knows everything about everybody else. At least everybody else knows everything about everybody. I don't know anything about anybody at all.

Biff, though, knows it all. When he's not opening doors, he can always be found on the intercom gossiping with the neighbors. Sometimes, when it's just a kid like Wil or me trying to get in or out, he doesn't even bother to get off the lobby phone to open the door. He just smiles and waves us through like a traffic cop. Then he goes back to his conversation. He never does that with adults though, and heaven forbid we complain about it to our parents, even when our arms are full of books or groceries and we could use a little help. If we do mention it, we get a sermon about becoming spoiled brats because we expect the same service as other human beings.

After we got outside, Wil and I waited with my mother while Biff waved at occupied cabs for her.

Biff finally attracted the attention of a taxi, but it was on the opposite side of the street and going the wrong way. We had to wait for the light to change so the cab could make a U-turn and pick Mama up in front of the building. I think Biff thought Mama's grief was too great for her to cross the street. The taxi was finally able to make its turn, but it had to cut off a bus to do it. The bus driver shouted something unprintable at the cab driver, and the cab driver shouted something equally pungent back. Then they gave each other a version of Biff's thumbs-up gesture, except with a different finger. That's how it is in New York. As long as no one gets physical about it all, everyone goes away a little happier.

As she got into the cab, Mama reminded me for the third time to go to my grandmother's apartment after school to check on her mail. Grandma was still at her house in the country, and while she was, it was my job to avoid postal buildup. I don't mind doing it. She has a very nice garden behind her brownstone, and sometimes I sit out there and do my homework.

Wil and I waved good-bye to Mama as the cab pulled away, and she returned our farewells through the back window. With that kind of parting, all she needed was a suitcase, and she could have been going to Europe for a year or two. It was all very touching. At least Biff looked touched; he even tried to give me a consoling pat on the head. When that didn't work, he tried to give Wil a consoling pat on the head, but Wil was too quick on his feet, so Biff wound up patting Wil's soccer ball instead. If soccer balls have feelings, I'm sure it felt lots better about everything.

Mama kept waving until the cab finally turned the corner. Wil complained that it had taken Biff forever to find an empty taxi, so we'd have to rush to school and he'd miss his chance to kick his soccer ball door to door. I can't say I minded that at all. It wasn't that I was against his kicking his soccer ball like some kind of fetish. What I minded is that he insisted on kicking his soccer ball at me until I kicked it back. I have my decorum to think about, but I often found myself walking down the street kicking a soccer ball like a little kid.

"It helps me practice," he complained every time I complained. "Don't you want to help me practice? Don't you want me to be a great athlete?"

"You never help me practice," I said, dodging the ball.

"Practice what?" he asked, rushing past me.

"Riding. Don't you want me to be a great athlete?"

"That's different," he said, because athletes who don't ride aren't sure that athletes who do are athletes in the first place. But they are. All you have to do is watch an athlete who doesn't ride trying to ride a horse to realize that.

Wil kicked the ball in my direction, but I athletically hopped over it. Wil chased past me and retrieved it with his toe. Then he nimbly

23

moved it with his feet between two people walking together.

"How could I help you?" he asked.

"You could muck out a stall, for instance. That would be a big help. You could clean tack if you'd like."

"You don't need a helper, you need a slave," he said, twirling the ball around on the sidewalk with the tip of his shoe.

Just then he kicked the ball to me, which is a lot better than kicking it at me. I kicked it back to him, and we continued that way until we were almost at school. Then we both stopped. We both had our reputations to think about. Wil didn't want his friends to see him kicking a soccer ball to a girl, and I didn't want my friends to see me kicking a soccer ball at all, especially in a new dress.

Wil and I walked the last block like two strangers who happened to be related. He occupied his mind with keeping the soccer ball poised in midair by kicking it straight up from one knee to the other. I occupied my mind with thoughts of Blue.

"What's wrong with you today?" Wil asked as we reached our school yard. "Are you upset about Daddy?" he asked.

"No," I answered. "I'm upset about my horse Blue."

"You mean last summer still bothers you?"

"No. This winter bothers me." I explained the situation to him just before we went into the building. I told him I hoped to convince our parents

24

to let me bring Blue to the city and board him at the stable where I take my jumping lessons.

"Now let me get this straight," he said, and put his soccer ball under his arm. "You expect our parents to pay for it?"

"I don't exactly expect it. You could say, I hope it."

"Well, good luck," he said sarcastically as two of his teammates showed up. Wil let the soccer ball drop to the ground, and suddenly I was in the middle of six enthusiastic feet all kicking at the same time. It wasn't easy, but I managed to escape without getting involved with the scramble of legs that suddenly broke out all around me.

"No, seriously," Wil shouted to me as I tried to pretend I was alone. "Good luck. I really mean it."

"Thanks," I said, because he sounded as if he really did mean it. One can never tell with one's little brother, but I was willing to give him the benefit of any doubts I had in mind.

# Chapter Three

When I walked into school that day, I was shaken to notice mostly everyone gawking at me. I wondered if I was wearing my new dress backwards. My mother said the buttons went down the front; but it looked to me as if they were supposed to go down the back. I'd decided to take her word for it, and now I was being gaped at! I'm not sure which was worse, thinking it was because of my dress or wondering if it was something else entirely.

It seemed to me the best thing to do was try not to call attention to the way I put my clothes on, so I faced the wall and walked to my locker sideways. That caused some quiet mumbling among my gawkers. It was a relief to reach my locker and face a familiar metal door. Of course, I was so curious about the situation in general that I forgot my combination and stood there in a trance for six minutes.

The first two numbers were just about to enter my mind when Marcie Anks drove them out again

27

by jabbing her finger into my shoulder by way of saying hello.

"Are we really going to that ridiculous soccer game?" she asked me, wrinkling her nose so I'd know that she wasn't thrilled at the prospect.

"I'm afraid so, Marcie," I said, carefully turning the dial of my lock to the numbers that suddenly popped into my head. "We have to. It's a family affair, and family is family."

"But I'm just a friend of the family. As a matter of fact, I'm not even that. I'm your friend."

"Marcie, do you remember when we were kids and used to sell lemonade and pretend we were sisters?"

"And you made me carry everything but the money box? Yes, it seems to me I do remember that."

"You were terrible in arithmetic and you know it. But, besides that, our pretending we were sisters made you at least a friend of the family. A friend who would go to a soccer game if her used-to-be-pretend sister asked her to."

"Okay, okay. I've had my dose of guilt. I want to go to the game. I'm looking forward to going to the game."

"You don't have to get carried away about it."

"As long as I'm pretending, I thought I'd pretend I was going to enjoy myself."

My lock finally decided to have mercy on me and practically fell open. I yanked the door open—it's the only way I can get it to move—and looked into my overstuffed locker. There was my math book. What a relief. For a while there, I thought it was lost. Then I would have had the pleasure of going to my mother for money to pay the school so they'd give me a new one. I could imagine her reaction.

"Well," she'd say, "if you can't take care of a math book, how on earth do you ever expect to take care of a horse?"

So I was happy to see that my math book was resting comfortably on my gym shorts and under a half box of cookies I'd forgotten about. I stuffed the book and the cookies into my backpack, so I could review them both during my morning study hall.

Marcie watched the cookies go into my backpack. She was just about to call halves on them when Sally Keeler came prancing down the hall to meet us. I say "prancing" because it's really the only way to describe the way Sally moves. She's a baton twirler, and twirls at all the games. Marcie says it's just so she can wear a short skirt and those cute white boots.

One thing everybody agrees on though—even me—is that Sally Keeler looks adorable prancing around the field. She must have heard about it, too, because lately she's given up normal walking entirely.

"Hi!" Sally said, reluctantly coming to a stop in front of us. She quickly locked her legs and thrust out her backside like a gymnast landing her dismount. That was her next most adorable look. I certainly didn't hold that against her. Sometimes I think it might be nice to look as adorable as she looks. Although, she does have to work at it, and

I prefer to stroll not prance when I'm not on a horse.

"That so totally cool game is Saturday," Sally said happily.

"It should be a good one," I said. "Wil thinks the other team is really good."

"And I bet Sally's twirling," Marcie said, a little sarcastically.

"And I bet you're not," Sally said back. "But you're going, aren't you? I mean you too, Marcie."

"Only to see you drop your baton," Marcie said, smiling sweetly.

"Now, Marcie," Sally purred. "I know if it weren't for people like you, there'd be no people like me, so in your own way, you're necessary too."

"That makes me feel lots better, Sally, but I think it's time for contemporary history." Marcie slipped her arm through mine and began dragging me down the hall to Mr. Rockbaund's history class.

"I just love your dress," Sally called after us. "Are you sure you're wearing it right?" Then she spun on her toes in the direction of her next class and pranced adorably off to the sound of a brass band somewhere in her head.

"Marcie," I whispered loudly as we went to our desks, "does this dress look funny to you?"

"I think it's kind of nice."

"I mean do you think I'm wearing it backwards?"

Marcie stopped walking and looked at me. "I don't think so," she said. "What do you mean?"

"I mean, are the buttons supposed to go down the back?"

"They look all right to me."

"Are you sure? They're not supposed to go down the back?"

"Well, I wouldn't want to spend the whole day sitting on a row of buttons. Yes, I'm sure you're wearing the dress right. Why do you ask?"

"It's just that I get the feeling everyone's staring at me. It must be my imagination."

"No it's not," Marcie said, leaning closer to me. "I think they're staring at you too."

"That really makes me feel a lot better. I think I liked it better when it was just my imagination. But why are they staring at me?"

"You mean you haven't heard? Didn't you watch *Rock News Week* on television this morning? I was being diplomatic, not mentioning it. I didn't know I was missing an opportunity to tell you something awful."

"We don't watch *Rock News* on television in the morning at my house. I'm not allowed to even turn the set on until my homework's done."

"Well, we're not that strict. The only time the TV isn't on in my house is when everybody's asleep, and even then, I'm not so sure."

"What were you being diplomatic about? And not mentioning?"

"It's all over school already. I thought you knew, and I was being your silent but loyal friend, pretending it had never happened, or even if it did, not letting it make a difference in our friendship."

31

"Marcie, what are you talking about?"

"Well," she said, putting the top of her head close to the bottom of my eyebrows because I'm taller, "I was watching *Rock News* while I had my breakfast this morning, and they ran some clips from the U-Haul concert you went to. One of the clips was of your father waving his arms around in the air in the middle of the band's big number. He seemed to be shouting your name."

"He wasn't waving his arms, Marcie. He was waving his shoe."

"His shoe! Is that what it was? My father said it looked like a bomb! Is he in prison?"

"It wasn't that serious, Marcie."

"If *Rock News* ever showed a videotape of my father waving his shoe around in the air shouting in the middle of a concert I'd think it was serious," Marcie replied reasonably. "But if you don't think so, that's okay."

# Chapter Four

"Young ladies," Mr. Rockbaund said to Marcie and me in his very tired patient voice, "you don't have to stand in my presence. Take your seats, just as the rest of the class has done. Make yourselves comfortable while you're not paying attention. We don't stand on ceremony here. I like to think we're all one informal family."

"Ask him if he wants to go to Saturday's game," Marcie whispered as we sat down.

Mr. Rockbaund took attendance, and then he began returning our graded papers. I'd done mine as a photo essay. When Mr. Rockbaund first assigned the paper, I asked if I could do one about the recent contemporary history of my summer camp and my horse Blue. Mr. Rockbaund said that a well-done photo essay of how I spent my vacation could perhaps be construed as an exercise in contemporary history, even though he wasn't quite sure how.

I agreed with him, and quoted that saying about a picture being worth a thousand words. Mr.

Rockbaund smiled and said it depended on the picture, but I had his permission to try.

It wasn't easy either. I showed, through several newspaper photographs mingled with my own snapshots, how my life at camp mirrored the goings on in the world at the time. For instance, while I was trying to get Blue over a jump fence in July, someone was trying to fly from New York to California on a gallon of gas. While we were petitioning Mr. Hildebrande for edible food, prisoners someplace were on strike for telephone privileges. It was all very symbolic and almost spooky just how caught up in world events I really was.

Luckily, in preparing the assignment, I had a newspaper from the summer. I'd used it to pack a set of souvenir glass tumblers from a horse show we'd gone to, and they were still in my trunk. Of course I had to iron the pages flat before I could use them. That caused the bottom of the iron to turn black, and Mama wasn't thrilled. I explained to her that it was for the cause of scholarship, and she said she'd keep that in mind the next time she had to press one of her silk scarves.

Personally, I thought it was worth it, especially the picture of the scandalous animal shelter that got closed down. It looked exactly like the bunkhouse I spent the summer in.

Mr. Rockbaund shuffled the papers neatly into a pile and walked up and down the aisles of the classroom distributing the compositions and announcing the grades as he went. He says it's the only fun he gets out of life. Sometimes it was enough to make one fall under one's seat.

"Sara, B. Jerome, B minus," he said quietly, saving his voice for the best and worst grades. All I was waiting for was mine. "Henry!" Mr. Rockbaund suddenly shouted. "C minus!"

Poor Henry. Mr. Rockbaund isn't exactly in love with Henry. In fact, some members of the class think he hates him. It isn't really Henry's fault. The problem is, Henry can walk on his hands farther than anyone else I've ever seen. He likes to do it every chance he gets. It's not unusual to see him walk into class that way. With a talent like that, it sometimes seemed unfair that he regularly got such low marks. On the other hand, it did sometimes seem to me that Henry just wasn't applying himself to anything other than walking on his hands. I know that's how most of the teachers felt about it. The only teacher who seems to appreciate him is our phys. ed. instructor.

"Jennifer, A!", Mr. Rockbaund said enthusiastically.

"Teacher's pet," Marcie whispered. Jennifer's a perfectly nice girl who's never gotten anything less than a B plus, and that sometimes gets on Marcie's nerves. "I think there's some favoritism being shown here," Marcie said, nodding her head so at least one of us would agree with what she said.

"Marcie," Mr. Rockbaund said with a huge smile, "B plus."

"What were you just saying, Marcie?" I asked.

"In my case," Marcie sniffed, "it's pure scholarship." And we both laughed.

"Mitchel, C plus, Joseph, F! And I don't have to remind you that's your second F in a row."

"It must be another of his creations," Marcie whispered.

Joe's very bright. He's an abstract artist and he likes to do things in an abstract way—including his homework assignments.

"At least he stapled his report together nicely," Marcie said, because I think she secretly likes Joe, and he borrowed her stapler for the occasion. "I think he deserves a better grade."

"Like what, for instance?"

"He could have given him an F plus. Then he could at least feel that he was improving."

Suddenly Joe spoke up. "Mr. Rockbaund," he said, "I'd like to protest my grade."

Mr. Rockbaund stopped handing out the papers and looked at Joe. "Joseph, I think I'm the one who should protest your grade. You handed in four nicely stapled pages in an attractive binder. But there was nothing on the pages."

"But you let Tiffin do a photo essay because it makes a statement."

How was I getting dragged into this?

"Well," Joe continued, "blank pages make a statement too."

"Yes, in a way they do," Mr. Rockbaund agreed. "If this were an art class, they very well might. But since this is contemporary history, do you know what statement they make to me?"

"Not exactly," Joe answered in a very quiet voice. "What statement do they make?"

"F, Joseph, loud and clear. F."

"But," Joseph protested, "doesn't neatness count?"

"Yes. I appreciate it. Alexander, C plus, Tiffin—"

I held my breath; there'd been only one A so far. Would there be any others? There had to be. I wouldn't be able to go near my mother with talk of Blue living in the city with anything less than an A on my side.

Here it comes, I thought. The moment of real truth—to Blue or not to Blue.

"A!"

I deserved it, if only for the care I took ironing the newspaper. Those weren't some last minute pictures just thrown together the night before the assignment and handed in. This was something more. I'd formed a photographic diary of last summer, and arranged them in an even nicer binder than Joseph's, and I drew a very nice horse on the cover, even though I'm not an artist and it came out looking as if it had only three legs. Blue, I thought, and hugged my paper, here you come—I hope.

"Sarabeth," Mr. Rockbaund called out, and looked at Sarabeth over the tops of his glasses, "B minus. You did a very nice job, Sarabeth. And you made it long too. But you said you were going to write about the history of gift giving and its current practice. Tips on shopping for bargains at Bloomingdale's is not exactly what we had in mind for the topic, is it?"

"It's exactly what I had in mind," Sarabeth said as she smiled at the B minus on her paper. "I'm going there right after school."

Mr. Rockbaund sighed and looked up at the ceiling without moving his head. It looked like his eyes were disappearing into his scalp. He barely had time to finish distributing the papers and give us our weekend assignment before the bell rang.

"Ah," Marcie gleamed, "one study hall, one lunch, and three more classes, and thus endeth a school week."

"Then, on to the weekend. What do you want to do Saturday night?"

"You mean after watching several wretched little boys running around in short pants all morning? Perhaps go home and throw up."

I knew how she felt, but I had no choice about the game. If I expected my mother to even listen to me about Blue, I had to appreciate Wil's efforts all over the place, and wave my A in front of her face. Then maybe I'd have a chance, and maybe Blue would too. In a way, it was now or possibly never.

My parents were entering their broken-family-guilt stage. The last time this happened, it lasted two weeks. That's why my new dress suddenly appeared. This time Mom had prepared in advance. She'd even bought Wil a soccer ball to add to his collection. His room is beginning to resemble Mr. Hildebrande's outhouse the time we filled it with pinecones.

I tried explaining the circumstances about Blue to Marcie several times and several ways as the day went by. She finally got the point, but wasn't entirely sympathetic. Marcie claims she doesn't get along with horses, and they don't get along with her.

I did try to get her interested in riding once,

and took her to the stable for a lesson. They put her on a lovely beginner horse called Technicolor. "Hello, horsey," she said to him as soon as she plopped safely into the saddle. That must have been more than he could stand, because he turned his head all the way round and bit her foot. It was just a little love nip really, hardly worth the bloodcurdling scream she let out. The poor horse was almost frightened to death. After all, it was just his horsey way of saying hello.

Marcie didn't take it that way though, and that little show of affection ended the lesson right there. I tried to explain to her that it was all a matter of attitude. At least, that's what my father always tells me about everything. Most times I'm not exactly sure what he's talking about, and Marcie felt the same way about it when I tried it on her.

She said that if anybody had an attitude problem, it was the horse. She showed me two bruised toes after they turned an interesting green, blue, and purple.

"Now," Marcie said, as she wiggled her multicolored foot in my face, "I know how that beast got its name."

# Chapter Five

My friend Tara was waiting for me outside school at the end of the day. She and I always walk home together. We're both latchkey kids, as they say. That means there's no one waiting for us with cookies and milk. In a way it's not so bad. We usually stop for a slice of pizza on our way, and if there's one thing I don't care for after pizza, it's cookies and milk.

"Did you see your father on television?" Tara asked happily. "He looked great."

"Thanks," I said. "You're the only one who seems to think so."

"Why do you say that? Lots of kids thought he looked great. I wish my father would take us to concerts and dance in the aisles."

"Tara, he wasn't dancing in the aisles. He was looking for us, remember?"

"Of course. But everybody I've talked to thinks he was dancing in the aisles."

"Well, didn't you tell them what happened?"

"Of course not," she answered. "Most of the people I talked to think he looked totally cool."

"And the rest? What did they think?"

"Oh, them," she said, snorting. "They think he looked totally looney."

"Thanks very much, Tara. That's just what I needed."

Tara laughed and took a pocket mirror out of her purse. She looked into it and frizzed up the front of her hair with her fingers. She's very much into the heavy metal music scene and dresses like her favorite band. They frizz up the front of their hair too. She says her total dream is to get one of those leather jackets they seem to wear day and night in all kinds of weather. She's been saving up for one. She's already ripped a new pair of jeans at the knees, and bought an electric guitar with an amplifier that can lift the roof off a building. Her parents allow her to play it only when they're not at home. She believes the man who lives upstairs from her must be a music fan too. She says he tries to keep time to her music by stamping on the floor.

"He's not very musical," she once told me. "He keeps missing the beat," and someday, she said, she expects the entire ceiling to fall on her bed. It's really too bad, because Tara wants to form a band, and hoped she'd found a drummer right in her own building. She offered me the job once she decided the person upstairs had no rhythm. I mentioned it to my father, but he only covered his face with both hands and moaned.

We passed Wil and his teammates on our way out of the school yard. They were going to practice for their big game, and Tara and I managed to avoid being used as substitute goal targets. Then we walked to the pizza shop, but I didn't have much of an appetite. All I could think about was Blue being led off somewhere to an awful fate, so Tara finished my slice for me while I drank my Coke.

Tara was very surprised, because usually I finish my own slice, except for the edge of the crust if it's too well done. She asked me what was wrong and I told her about Blue. She said it was something of a coincidence, because the jacket she wanted to buy was actually made of horsehide. Well, I almost fainted onto my paper plate. That was about the last thing I wanted to hear. Just then, two members of the school band walked into the pizza parlor, and one of them was wearing a black leather jacket with fringe.

"Oh, Blue," I said, and from out of nowhere, a great big tear came oozing silently out of my eye, rolled down my cheek, and plopped loudly into my cup of melting ice. Tara reached across the table and squeezed my hand.

"Don't worry," she consoled. "When I buy a jacket, I'll make sure the leather came from a cow." That didn't make me feel much better at all. I didn't understand why anyone had to wear leather jackets in the first place. Not even if they came from a cow. I once heard that you could make leather out of soybeans, I think. That seemed like a fine idea. Although maybe some people feel the same way about soybeans as I feel about horses, or even temporarily, cows, but I've never met them.

Once though, when a new fried chicken restaurant opened near my school, a man was picketing with a sign protesting cruelty to poultry. His sign said he was a vegetarian and everyone should be. The manager of the new place came out onto the sidewalk looking very upset.

"What about cruelty to vegetables?" he asked the person with the sign. "Don't you think they have feelings too?" he demanded to know. The picketer looked momentarily stunned at the thought. It certainly gave me something to think about as I munched my pizza that day. I wondered what sort of agony the tomatoes had gone through on their way to my slice. Did the wheat that went into the flour that made the dough leave any relatives behind? That night, my mother put a bowl of salad in front of me and I almost burst into tears. It was enough to ruin my appetite for days.

When Tara and I got up to leave, and as we passed the boy in the jacket, I asked him what it was made of.

"Leather," he said, as if I'd asked the dumbest question in the world. I was hoping he'd say soybeans, because by then I was over my morbid concern for vegetable welfare. Besides, he was cute, and maybe we had a humane interest in common.

"What kind of leather?" I demanded hopefully. He looked at me, then at his friend, and shrugged his shoulders. I was about to ask him to take it off and check the inside for clues, but Tara dragged me out the door. At least I made some sort of impression on him, because he twirled his finger on the side of his temple. I chose to believe that meant he was crazy about me.

Tara and I walked together quietly for a block or so. Usually we chat, but almost every thought in my head started with the word Blue. Tara reached into her bag and took out her pocket tape player. I guess all the gloom gave her a craving for music. She slipped earphones onto her head and sang along to her favorite band. How could anyone be happy, and singing no less, at a time like this?

We stopped at the library on our way home. I had to return a book I'd borrowed and Tara wanted to get one. Next to pizza after school, stopping at the library is one of my favorite things to do. Usually that is. It's fun to browse through the long rows of books, and generally there's a friend or two to run into. That day, several kids from my school were there, and one of them asked me if my father was a musician. Maybe it was my imagination, but I think she snickered a little halfway through the question.

"No," I answered, a little testily I suppose. You don't have to be a musician to go to a concert and look for your daughter and appear on *Rock News*. Although I suppose it helps. If he had been a musician and featured on *Rock News* the way he'd been, everybody would have ooohed and aaahed about how famous he was getting. They probably would have even asked me to get his autograph or something.

Tara got her book, and my browsing mood had

just been destroyed, so we left. We said so long when we reached my grandmother's house. It's right near Central Park, and I sometimes wished I lived there so I could get to the stable more easily. Tara gave me a soulful look and said that everything would be all right. Then she frizzed up her bangs again, and turned up the volume on her headset.

I stood in front of my grandmother's for a minute or two watching Tara until she reached the corner. I guess I was getting used to seeing people off or something. I looked in my backpack, and found the keys to my grandmother's apartment. Granny used to live in the whole house a long time ago when my grandfather was alive, but that was before I was born. Now though, she says it's much too big for just her, her ancient chauffeur Old Tim, and Edna the maid, who's even older than both of them put together—if that's possible.

None of them is exactly thrilled at the thought of climbing too many stairs, so Grandma converted the garden and parlor floors into one apartment, and the top three floors into another, which is rented for a small fortune to a famous actor and his latest wife. He's been married at least three times since he moved into the building. And he plays such a loving husband on television too. It just goes to show, you never can tell. On the other hand, maybe he is a loving husband, right up to the divorce. He's very good-looking, and always nice to me, and makes a big fuss over Grandma. She pretends not to like it, but I know she does. She always asks him to dinner between wives.

The arrangement seems to have worked out pretty well for Grandma, and I'm glad of it. Not that she's there much to begin with. She spends most of her time in the country. It's better for everybody concerned. Tim is so ancient he hardly even drives the car when they're in the city anymore. My grandmother drives it instead. Old Tim just sits in the passenger seat of the antique Packard in case Granny has to park at a fire hydrant. I wouldn't be surprised if she did the housework while the maid stayed in bed. My grandmother's very active for her age. That particular day, I wished that she was there so I could ask her about Blue. She might understand. She always does, most times.

I considered calling her on the phone to discuss it with her, but she's gotten a little hard of hearing, especially on the phone, and shouts "What?" a lot. It's amazing to me that she and Tim can hold any kind of conversation at all, because he shouts "What?" a lot too. Maybe that's why they get along.

On my way into the apartment, I checked her mailbox. There was a letter to me from her, reminding me to water the azaleas in the garden. I wondered for just a moment whether maybe my father was right about flowers after all. Somehow, plastic azaleas didn't sound quite the same.

I went into the apartment through the ground floor entrance and couldn't help thinking that I was more than a latchkey kid. These days, I was a two latchkeys kid. If my father ever settled down in a place of his own, I might even become a three latchkeys kids. That's a lot of places not to have cookies and milk in.

I walked through Grandma's and put my books on the small breakfast table that faces her garden. It's not actually the kind of garden you might expect to find if you live in the country. This is a city garden, with bricks where the dirt should be, a few carefully placed trees, several wrought iron benches, chairs, and three small round tables with folded umbrellas sticking up through a hole in their middles. It's very pretty in its own way though, quiet and peaceful, as if the city were far away.

After turning off the burglar alarm and unlocking the sliding glass door that leads out back, I filled a watering can and did my duty to the flowers. There's a small potting shed out there that two geraniums have all to themselves.

It was such a lovely afternoon that I sat at one of the tables in the garden for a while. I looked up at the nearby houses wondering who lived behind all those windows. Naturally, this being a city garden, several of the apartment building windows had people behind them, looking down at me looking up at them. Granny's trees had lost most of their leaves, and my privacy along with them, so I raised the umbrella of the table and enjoyed the afternoon air.

It occurred to me that it might be a good idea to telephone my camp friend Lily. What with watering the azaleas, her name popped into my mind. Granny said I should make myself at home provided I cleaned up any mess I made. That seemed to me to include telephone privileges, even if it was long distance. I lowered the umbrella and went back into the house. I closed and locked the sliding glass doors and turned the intruder alarm back on. Then I called Lily in Massachusetts.

"Tiffin!" Lily said to me when she answered her phone. "I was just trying to call you." Isn't that strange how things like that happen? "Wait just a minute," she said. "I just got home from school and I'm eating a peanut butter sandwich, and all of it's stuck to the roof of my mouth."

It was hard to understand what she was saying. But having spent a summer with her, I knew what she sounded like with peanut butter stuck to the roof of her mouth. The next sound I heard was that of her phone being dropped onto the table.

I waited a few seconds, wondering how much Lily's chewing problem was costing my grandmother. Finally she got back on the line.

"I'm so glad you called," she said, clear as a bell. "I just got off the phone with Mr. Hildebrande. I had to ask him about my horse's shoes." Lily had taken her camp horse home with her for the winter, and naturally Mr. Hildebrande had sent him there wearing his old shoes, so the first thing she had to do was pay for a farrier to put on new ones. Her parents wanted to know how often they were going to have to do that little chore. The answer was, more often than they expected.

"He said," she continued, almost breathlessly. Maybe, I thought, she's exhausted from battling her peanut butter. "That today's the last day he can wait to hear from anybody about Blue."

"What do you mean, the last day?" I asked her, suddenly breathless myself.

"I don't know exactly," she answered. "But it sounded grim, and I was afraid to ask."

"You mean . . ." I said, afraid to hear the rest of the sentence come out of my mouth.

"I think so," she answered, reading my thoughts. "If you're going to do anything about Blue, you'd better do it soon," she warned. Even without her coming right out and saying it, I knew what she was talking about. If someone, namely me, didn't agree to take Blue—and fast—he was an immediate candidate for horsey heaven.

"Oh, Lily," I moaned, "what am I going to do?"

"Have you spoken to your parents yet?"

"Now's not exactly a good time," I tried to explain.

"Well," Lily suggested, "if I were you, I'd at least call Mr. Hildebrande now. Otherwise, you may be too late."

*Too late.* Her words sank into my ears and I could almost feel tears forcing themselves up my throat. Lily gave me Mr. Hildebrande's private telephone number, and then we hung up so I could call him. I knew Grandma wouldn't mind. At least that's what I told myself as I dialed.

I won't go into the exact conversation I had with Mr. Hildebrande. Mainly because I don't remember it word for word, and by that time, the tears had gotten past my throat, skipped my nose, and went straight for my eyes. All I know is that he said today was the day or else. He was very nice about it. I was surprised at what a human

**50**

being he sounded like. He said there'd be other horses to ride, and how it was better for everybody concerned, including Blue. I just didn't see how that could be. All I could picture was Blue being led into a van, all trusting and sweet, and before I knew it, I was agreeing to take Blue for the winter. It was as if someone else was doing the talking. I mean, it was me, and I could hear myself saying, "Yes, ship him to me here in the city."

He sounded very happy to hear that, if only for Blue's and my sake. "Have you cleared it with your parents?" he asked, and that voice that had said, yes, ship him, only a few seconds before suddenly mumbled Yes. It sounded a little muffled, but it said yes. I know, because I heard it. Then, Mr. Hildebrande actually offered to pay Blue's carfare. I was stunned! The situation was even more desperate than I imagined.

Mr. Hildebrande said he had to leave for Florida that very day, but he'd tell the van driver to contact me to make the final arrangements. The words "final arrangments" sounded very final, but at least they weren't the final final arrangements for Blue that I'd been afraid of.

"Can he call you on Monday?" Mr. Hildebrande asked, and once again I said yes. Monday was less than three days away, practically a lifetime. Who knows, I told myself, maybe by then I'd win the lottery or something, although I'm too young to buy a ticket. Maybe my parents would win the lottery, although they don't gamble at all.

I gave him my grandmother's telephone number,

and asked him to have the man who was going to van Blue call me there late Monday afternoon. He wished me a happy winter and said he was looking forward to seeing me next summer, because I was one of his favorite campers. I happen to know he says that to all the campers who intend to return, but it was nice to hear anyway. I told him Camp Off-the-Wall was the best camp I'd ever been to, and that made him happy too. Of course I didn't refer to it that way. The real name of the place is Chucalucup, but the nickname we all gave it describes it much better. I also left out the part about its being the only camp I'd ever been to. Then we hung up.

I don't know which I felt more: guilty for having told a lie about clearing it already with my parents, or relieved for having saved Blue from a terrible fate. I don't like telling lies, and it's something I never do, except maybe if a friend of mine asks whether or not her dress is nice or something, and it isn't. But I don't like doing it. But this was to save Blue's life, I told myself, and sat next to the phone feeling bad and good all mixed up together.

# Chapter Six

"Why on earth did you do that?" I asked myself ten times as I sat by Granny's phone and watched the day slowly start to get dark. "To save Blue," I answered myself ten times. "Now what are you going to do?" I asked myself. "I don't know," I responded.

I called my father's office. I thought maybe he'd understand, but he was in with a patient and couldn't be disturbed. My mother's office said she'd gone to a political meeting with her friend Arthur. When I called my grandmother, we had, on top of everything else, a bad connection. All we got to say to each other was, "What?" until finally we gave up, and she said she'd see me in the city. She was coming into town in a few days to give a party in her apartment for my mother's candidacy. She said she'd talk to me then about whatever it was I wanted to talk about. My problem was that I needed money now just so Blue could poke his head into the stable near Central Park. I wasn't even thinking about whether he'd need new shoes or not. He could go barefoot for a while, I reasoned. It would do his legs good. After all, horses aren't born with iron rings on their feet.

I left my grandmother's house and walked home to mine very slowly. It's not too far, but the blocks seemed particularly long that day. Wil was just coming home from soccer practice and we met each other in front of our building.

"What's wrong with you?" he asked. "You look awful."

"Thanks, Wil," I responded. "I feel worse."

Biff was on the house phone for a change and waved us in through the front door. I guess he thought I looked awful too because he gave me several sympathetic nods and a thumbs-up gesture. He probably thought I was feeling bad about our domestic situation. In a way I was. How was I ever going to break the news to my family that we were about to get a new thousand-pound member?

On the way up in the elevator, I turned to Wil and blurted out what had happened. All he had to say about it was, "Uh oh."

That's just how I felt about it too. The first thing I did when we got into our apartment was to count all the money in my bank. It's a very nice little thing I'd gotten for one of my birthdays, and was once a post office box. I dialed the combination and hoped for a rush of money. Happily, it contained more than I'd expected. Unhappily, it contained less than I needed. I fished through my desk drawer and found the savings book that Grandma had given me. There was

54

enough there to take care of Blue for a while anyway, but that was supposed to be my college fund, and I knew that no one would let me touch it. That's the problem with having money when you're a kid: no one will let you touch it. In any case, I'd need everybody's permission to get to it, and I knew how unlikely that was.

I tried calling my father again, this time at the university club, but he wasn't there.

My mother didn't come home that evening until past my bedtime. I was going to wait up for her, but sleep got the better of me.

The next day was Wil's soccer game, and with all the rushing around that morning, I didn't have a chance to talk to anybody about anything. When I told Mama I wanted to talk to her about something, she said I should wait until after the game. She had to help drive the equipment for Wil's team to the park, and rushed right out of the house to meet Arthur and his car. Marcie came by for me in time to go to the game, and we walked to the Sheep Meadow in Central Park. On the way, I told Marcie what had happened, and she said the same thing as Wil had, "Uh oh." So far it was unanimous.

When we got to the park, Sally Keeler and her baton were already there. She was busy prancing for the benefit of the assistant coach of the team Wil was playing. He was cute, I have to admit that. Sally joined Marcie and me on the sidelines long enough to catch her breath.

"Isn't he adorable?" she asked, and sighed in

the direction of the assistant coach of the enemy team.

"Not as adorable as you are, Sally," Marcie answered.

The game started and I forgot my troubles for a little while. Wil was awfully good. He ran up and down the field kicking the ball and making goals for his team. Sally, meanwhile, pranced up and down the field, twirling her baton better than I'd ever seen her do, and generally making points for her cause. It was very exciting—Wil's performance, I mean.

My father arrived slightly late and clutching a camera. He took lots of pictures of the game, and of my mother shaking hands with everybody who looked like a voter. Her friend Arthur was her official unofficial campaign manager, and led her from group to group introducing her as a potential candidate who wasn't really interested in running for office, but who would serve if called on. Then my mother, looking very civic-minded, would shake everyone's hand, and my father would take a picture. When he wasn't snapping and she wasn't shaking, they stood together talking and laughing as if they were living under the same roof. It all had something to do with politics, I think. We were the most happy looking broken family I'd ever seen.

After the game, Sally came to stand with Marcie and me again. She was panting from all the work she'd done.

"You looked great out there, Sally," I told her,

because actually she had. She smiled happily and said thanks.

"All pranced-out, are you, Sally?" Marcie asked.

"Never." Sally smiled and straightened into her gymnast pose as she saw the assistant coach of the other team headed in our direction.

"Look!" Sally said. "He's coming this way!"

Not only was he coming our way, he was coming directly over to us.

"Do you want us to leave, Sally?" Marcie asked.

"That won't be necessary," Sally answered. "Just try to look inconspicuous and grateful to be in my presence."

"We always look inconspicuous," Marcie said in her most cutting tone of voice. "It's just our fate, I guess. However, I'm not sure about the grateful part. My parents tell me I'm the most ungrateful child they've ever known. Tiffin, are you trying to look inconspicuous?"

"I'm trying as hard as I can," I said.

The assistant coach kept walking straight toward us. When he was just a few feet away, Marcie dropped to both knees, stretched her arms out, and began salaaming up and down from the waist in the general direction of Sally's feet.

"That won't be necessary," Sally said graciously. "You may rise."

Sally put on her most dazzling smile for the assistant coach's benefit. He came up to us, smiled back at her, looked down at Marcie, and held out his hand to help her to her feet. Then he started talking to me.

"Hi," he said, "didn't I see you ride in a horse show last spring?"

I thought Sally was going to pass out on the spot. Her body actually relaxed its pose and she stood there with one hand on her hip. It was the first time I'd seen her in a normal posture in ages.

"Well, I was in a horse show last spring," I said. "At the stable on Eighty-ninth Street."

"I thought so," he said. "I had to leave before it ended. How did you make out?"

"I placed third," I said. "But it was a rented horse." The two riders who placed ahead of me were much older—one was a grown man—and they were both riding their own horses.

I didn't mention that, on account of Wil and some of his teammates, it was lucky I hadn't been disqualified altogether. They came to the show to cheer me on, and that's exactly what they did. "Rah, rah, rah," they chanted, "Sis boom bah. Tiffin, Tiffin. You'll go fah!" That's not exactly horse show etiquette, and I thought the judge would throw us all out. Happily for me, he settled on giving me long stony looks all through my ride. But there was no point in bringing that all up now, in the face of the cute assistant coach.

"No kidding," he said. "That's terrific. I thought you were excellent. When's your next show?"

"There's one scheduled for next month," I answered, in the high squeaky voice I always seem to acquire when I'm flustered.

"Maybe I'll see you there. If I don't, good luck

in advance. By the way, someone told me that player number five is your brother. Is that so?"

"Yes," I said, happy for once to admit a family relationship between Wil and me.

"I guess athletic talent runs in the family." He smiled. "Keep up the good work."

"Th-thanks," I stammered.

He smiled again and said so long.

"Move over, Sally," Marcie said. "I think I want to faint."

"He's not as cute close up," Sally snorted indignantly. Then she stiffened up nicely into the Sally I knew, and pranced off.

"Well," Marcie said, "maybe there's something to this horse business after all."

Mom helped Wil and his team load their equipment into Arthur's car, while Arthur told everyone who would listen that this was just one further example of Mom's public mindedness. Then she shook hands with everybody again, Daddy took more pictures, and I congratulated Wil on his team's win and his performance. He was very gracious about it.

"It just comes naturally," he said. Then he and his teammates went off noisily together.

My father joined Marcie and me, and took our picture as we watched Mom and Arthur drive away with the equipment. Marcie looked at her watch.

"Yipes," she said. "I'm going to be late."

"Where are you going?" I asked. I'd thought we were going to spend the afternoon together.

"My dentist," she groaned. "I have to have my braces tightened."

"Good luck," I said.

"You too," she said, and winked. We both knew she was talking about my situation with Blue.

"I guess that leaves the two of us," my father said as we watched everyone leave. "I hear you tried to call me yesterday."

"Yes. I wanted to talk to you."

"Good," he answered. "Let's have some lunch."

That sounded good to me. Maybe we'd go to a restaurant someplace and he'd have a Bloody Mary and be in a mellow, money spending mood. That's how I came to own a saddle the last time he and my mother separated. He'd taken me to the Devon horse show so we could spend some quality time together. That particular day, we had lunch between events and afterwards, as we walked past the saddler's booth, my father suddenly asked me if I needed a saddle. Since I already had a balloon and a souvenir tee shirt, I gulped and quickly said yes.

Maybe history could repeat itself for Blue's sake. I was prepared to wait for just the right time to bring the matter up. Sometime, I thought, in those pleasurable few minutes between finishing lunch and the arrival of the check.

We started to walk out of the park together, when Daddy stopped in his tracks.

"Look, there's a hot dog vendor," he said happily, because my father isn't exactly the biggest spend-thrift in the world.

"A hot dog for lunch?" I complained. Not that

**60**

there's anything wrong with a hot dog for lunch. There just wasn't much of a chance that Dad would grow mellow about money over a can of soda.

"Not a hot dog, Tiffin. You can have two."

What could I say? It was the only offer I'd had all day.

"Daddy," I said, after we got our hot dogs and sat on a bench, "what would you say if I told you I could get a free horse to ride all winter."

"Why," he said and stopped chewing, "I'd say that was wonderful." I think he was figuring that maybe "free horse" meant free jumping lessons as well as a rent-free horse to ride.

"And all we have to do is pay for board."

"Why," he said and swallowed, "I'd say that was terrible." My father may be a little thrifty, but he's definitely not stupid. He might not know the exact numbers involved, but he could figure out that boarding your own horse is more expensive than renting a horse to ride.

"But, Daddy," I began to protest, "it's Blue. And I can have him all winter."

"Did your mother put you up to this?" he asked, losing his appetite and looking sadly at his remaining hot dog.

"No. She doesn't know anything about it yet."

"Good," he said, "and when you speak to her about it, please don't mention that you mentioned it to me."

"But, Daddy," I said, "if I don't take Blue, and right away, he's going to . . . die." I almost sobbed into my sauerkraut.

"Tiffin, sweetheart," Daddy said, and looked at me very seriously. "You're very young, but you must understand. All things die," he said quietly. "But, in a way they don't really die." Then he very understandingly told me about how everything is made up of atoms and molecules and matter, and how atoms and molecules and matter never die. They just change form. So Blue wasn't really going to die, even though all things die. He was just going to change form, and in a way, live forever, just like everything else. "Do you see what I mean?" he asked as tenderly as he could when in danger of spending money.

In a way I understood. Partially because he told me the same thing when my gerbil, Trigger, changed form, in a way. All I knew then was that I had an empty gerbil cage on my hands. As a matter of fact, when that happened, my parents wanted to give the cage to our neighbor's child, who had just gotten a gerbil in its original form. I objected at the time and said that as long as the gerbil wasn't really dead, we should keep the cage for its molecules. We didn't, though. My parents said I really didn't understand just what they were trying to tell me. That's nothing new though, and the next thing I knew, Trigger's atoms were without a home.

We sat there for a few minutes in silence as the hot dog bun got soggy in my hands. I looked at the half-eaten frankfurter sticking out and wondered what its atoms had been in a previous life. Daddy put his arm around my shoulder and gave me a squeeze and a kiss on my head. Two ladies who were walking by turned around, and gave him a strange look as they passed. Then they began to whisper to each other.

"It's all right," he called out after them. "She's my daughter."

"Hmmph," one of them said, because, these days everybody's on the lookout for everything, especially in Central Park.

"Gosh," Dad said suddenly and looked at his watch. "Look at the time."

"Do you have a dentist's appointment too?" I asked.

"No, but maybe I still have time to make one."

That's my Dad for you. He'd rather go to the dentist than talk about money. That at least is covered by his medical insurance.

# Chapter Seven

My father walked me home to my building. Biff was standing outside and curled his lip at him, but opened the door for me with a lot of understanding in his eyes.

I went upstairs and did my homework, and a few hours later, Marcie came over. Wil was going to have a victory dinner with his team, and Mama was making political rounds with Arthur. Marcie and I watched television, played Monopoly, and ordered a pizza with extra cheese. That's one good thing about living in the middle of the city. You can have all sorts of food delivered right to your door.

After Marcie left, Wil came home and ate a piece of leftover pizza, which he heated in the microwave oven. I personally don't like microwaved pizza because it always comes out tasting like soft rubber. He yawned a lot and then went to bed.

Mama came home very late, massaging her hand-shaking hand. I think it was worn out from being so sociable for the good of society. I told her I wanted to talk to her about something terribly important, a matter of life or death.

"Can't it wait till morning?" she asked wearily, and went to soak in the tub.

The next morning, Wil left early to practice with his team and Mama and I were alone. Now was the time to bring up Blue.

"Hey, Mom?" I asked, getting kind of cozy about it, because my mother likes it when we're close and confidential about things that really matter. "Can I talk to you?"

If there's one thing my mother likes, it's when I ask if I can talk to her about something, unless she's tired or busy, which is most of the time. When she's not tired or busy, she clears everything aside and gives me her undivided attention. What she cleared aside this time was a stack of clean eyelet-trimmed sheets that had just come back from the laundry. Actually, they weren't in anybody's way in the first place, but moving something from one place to another was part of getting ready for our mother-daughter talk.

"Just let me get these out of the way," she said, and picked up the neatly piled sheets. I picked up my history report and followed her into her bedroom. I sat on her bed while she stacked the sheets in the armoire against the wall. Usually I just sit on the floor and she sits in the wooden rocking chair that Grandma gave her. It's next to her bed, and she likes to rock slowly while we talk. It's much more homey that way. Today though, my entire body was still aching from sitting on the ground through Wil's game. It needed the comfort of something soft for a while.

"Tiffin, dear," Mama said when she was finished sorting her sheets.

I stiffened a little, because whenever she says, Tiffin, dear, I know it's the introduction to a complaint.

"Tiffin, dear," she repeated, as if I hadn't heard her the first time. "That bed is freshly made, and you know Mommy doesn't like anyone to sit on a freshly made bed." Sitting on freshly made beds is one of my father's favorite things to do.

Reluctantly, I got up and eased my aching body to the floor. Mama sat in her rocking chair and slowly began to rock.

"What did you want to talk to me about?" she asked in her most concerned tone of voice. These little talks are very important to her; she gets a lot out of them.

"First of all," I said, handing her my A paper, "my history report."

"Good heavens," she said, before looking at the mark. "You didn't fail, did you?" If there's one thing I appreciate, it's a vote of confidence.

"Fail?" I protested. "I got an A!"

"An A?!" she exclaimed. I don't know why she was all that surprised. After all, it has happened before. Not many times, I admit, but it has happened. Maybe she was just trying to appreciate it a lot so it would happen more often.

"An A!" she said again, as if I hadn't just heard her. Then she hugged me. It was a little awkward, because she had to stop rocking and lean over double to do it. She wound up embracing my ears, while I settled for a squeeze of her knees.

We clutched each other for a few minutes, and then Mama straightened up, told me how happy I'd made her, got up from her chair, and walked out of the room. As far as she was concerned, we'd had our little talk and she felt a hundred percent better about everything. I, on the other hand, was left sitting on the floor with my mouth open.

I waited for her to come back into the bedroom. After a few minutes, it dawned on me that she had no intention of doing so. It took me a few seconds to scramble to my feet and follow her into the kitchen.

"Mama," I said, "there's still something I want to talk to you about."

"Oh, I'm sorry, dear. I thought we were finished. What is it you want to talk about?" For a while there, I thought I would have to follow her back into the bedroom. Instead, she looked quickly around the kitchen for something to clear out of the way. Nothing was in the way to begin with, so I sat at the table while Mama refilled a salt shaker and put it on the spice rack. Then she came and sat across the table from me.

"It's about Blue," I said.

"Blue what?" she asked.

"My horse Blue. From camp."

"Did he sit on someone?" She chuckled, referring to Blue's habit of sitting down when he wasn't supposed to. I was happy to hear her able to laugh at it now. She wasn't too thrilled the time it happened when I was riding him.

"Not that I know of, Mama. But he's in trouble. I got a letter from camp. All the horses have been placed for the winter. Except Blue. No one wants to take him because of his little quirks."

"Sitting down with a rider in the saddle is more than just a little quirk, dear. I would say that counts as a flaw." She laughed again. I'm not sure whether she was making a pun on the word "flaw" for "floor." If she was I didn't think it was funny, but she was having a wonderful time.

"Mama, please, I'm talking about a matter of life and death."

"I know how sensitive you are about horses, Tiffin. But don't you think you're being a little melodramatic about it?"

"Mama, Mr. Hildebrande has to go to Florida, and if he can't find a home for Blue until camp starts again, we may have to change Blue's name to glue."

"Oh, I see," she said quietly. "But what can we do about it?"

"We can take him for the winter," I explained quickly.

"Take him where?"

"Here."

"Take him here?" she asked, slightly astonished.

"I don't mean here in the apartment. I mean here in the city. We can board him at the stable."

With that, Mama got up and poured peppercorns into the pepper mill. At least we were prepared to season any occasion. Nobody spoke for a minute or two. The only sound was the rattle of peppercorns preparing to meet their fate. Then she put the large wooden grinder on the shelf next to the salt.

"Mr. Hildebrande will van him to us for nothing," I said quickly. "And we don't have to pay for Blue either. Just for his board, vet, and shoeing," I said, even more quickly. "And then, this coming summer, Mr. Hildebrande will van him back to the camp. Lots of kids from camp have taken their horses for the winter."

Mama came back to the table. She didn't sit down though. She just looked at me with her most reasonable expression, and I knew what was coming. She was going to say no, but very reasonably.

"Tiffin, darling," she said. Reasonably. "Lots of kids from camp don't live in the city. A horse in New York. I just don't see how it's possible."

"But, Mama," I pleaded, "it is possible. We can rent the cheapest stall at the stable. I'll take care of him. I can ride him in Central Park. And it won't cost much more than it costs now every time I have to rent a horse for my lessons."

"How much more?" she asked.

"Not much," I said. "Only about twice as much," I whispered.

I guess I didn't whisper low enough, because Mama gulped when she heard that. Then she got up from the table and looked around the room again. I expected her to clear the refrigerator into the hall.

"I'll do everything," I said. "You can apply my

allowance towards the board bill. I'll get more A's at school. I'll go to all Wil's games. I'll even stop sitting on your bed."

"Did your father put you up to this?" she asked.

"No," I answered. That's all my parents seem to have on their minds sometimes.

"Have you spoken to him about it?" she asked, because my Mom's no fool.

"Well . . ." I hesitated.

"And he told you not to mention having spoken to him to me."

"Well . . ." I hesitated again.

"I thought so," she said, although I don't know what good that was going to do anyone, especially poor Blue. Mama and I looked at each other without speaking. I attempted to look deserving. Finally she said very familiar words to me.

"I'll think it over."

That meant she was willing to think it over until I forgot about it.

"Now then," Mama said, brightening up as she changed the subject, "grandmother is holding a small reception for me on Tuesday. She's invited several influential people and some members of the press so I can meet them."

"Are you going to shake hands with everybody again?"

"Probably." She chuckled. "Your father will be there. Wil, too."

"Are we going to be one big happy family again?" I asked.

"Just for the day," she said and smiled. "What are you going to wear?"

71

"I'll go in mourning," I answered sadly, because that's the kind of mood I was in. "Uh, Mama," I began, knowing I'd have to tell her about my conversation with Mr. Hildebrande, "there's something else I have to tell you—"

Just as I was about to blurt it out, our intercom rang. Biff announced that we were getting a visitor. It was Arthur. He and my mother were going to meet even more people at yet another function. That ended our heart-to-heart talk right there. She wasn't always this busy. Just since she went into politics.

Arthur rang our doorbell and I went to let him in, while my mother went back into her bedroom to dress for the day.

"Hello, sunshine," Arthur said, and then looked closely at the expression on my face. "What's wrong?" he asked quietly.

"The world's coming to an end," I answered.

"Oh, is that all," he said, trying to cheer me up. "It's come to an end for me lots of times." I went back to the table and sat down.

Arthur joined me, prepared to listen. He's very nice really, and has known me since I was born. In fact he knew my mother even before my father did. They're very good friends, and sometimes, it's easier to talk to someone you're not actually related to.

"Look," Arthur said, "I know something that will make you smile." And then he wiggled his ears. I don't know how he does it, but he can sometimes get them flapping practically like an elephant. It always worked on me when I was growing up and feeling not too happy about this or that. No matter how bad I felt about something, Arthur could wiggle his ears at me until finally I'd laugh and feel better about things.

This time though, nothing could make me feel much better, not even Arthur's ears fanning the breeze.

He wiggled and wiggled until he got red in the face. "This must be serious," he said finally. "My ear muscles are all worn out, and you're still frowning."

"It's not your fault," I said. "I just don't think that works on me anymore."

"Wow, now I really feel old," he said. "You've passed the ear wiggle stage, the end of an era." Then he let his head collapse limply so that his chin touched his chest. I don't know why, but it made me giggle for an instant.

"Did I hear a giggle?" he asked, raising his head. "Do I see the beginning of a smile?"

"Not really," I answered. "It's about Blue."

"You mean your horse from camp? Did he sit on someone?"

"No, and that's just what my mother asked."

"What's that they say about great minds thinking alike?" he teased. When he saw I wasn't looking any happier, he said, "Come on now. Tell old Uncle Arthur what the problem is." He's not really my uncle, but that's how he likes to think of himself. I told him about Blue's predicament, and by now I was getting a little tired of repeating it to everybody in the world. I thought maybe I might write it down on small cards and just hand them out to anybody who asked. There's a man on the subway who does that. Not about Blue I mean, about himself. He doesn't seem to be able to speak or hear, so he goes from person to person and gives them a little card explaining his problem. You're supposed to give him money. If you do, he lets you keep the card, which has the hand sign alphabet on one side. If you don't he takes the card back, and gives you a dirty look.

Arthur listened carefully to what I had to say. "I see," he said, every time I paused to take a breath. When I finally finished telling him about Blue's upcoming catastrophe, he said, "I see," again, and rubbed his chin with his fingers. "Give me a couple of days to think about it," he said and rubbed his chin some more. "I'll see what I can do."

Arthur has a lot of influence with my mother, so his saying he'd see what he could do counted for something. The part that worried me was the couple of days he mentioned. I had to talk to Mr. Hildebrande's van driver the very next day. If I couldn't tell him to deliver Blue, I had the feeling it would all be over by the time Arthur was finished thinking about it.

"But—" I began to say there was a further problem, when my mother came out of the bedroom prepared to pursue her career. What could be better than telling her about the phone conversation I'd had with Mr. Hildebrande while Arthur was there? She was always understanding, but when Arthur was around, she was super-understanding.

"Have to go now, sweetheart," she said as I

opened my mouth. "Make sure you have lunch. Do your homework, and keep up the good work." She gave me a kiss, a squeeze, and a loving look. Then she headed for the door with Arthur right behind her.

"Don't worry," he turned to me and said, and winked for a second. "It's all going to be fine. Keep your chin up."

Then he wiggled his ears at me one more time, and they both hurried away.

# Chapter Eight

Arthur's reaction to my problems made me feel a little better. If anyone could convince my mother of anything, it was Arthur. He's a lawyer too, and I guess they know how to talk to each other. I went to the phone immediately to call Mr. Hildebrande. All I needed was a few more days, and things might work out the way I hoped. That wasn't so much to ask, considering a horse's life was at stake. There just doesn't seem to be much room in the world for a sometimes lame horse with all times weird habits.

It wasn't Blue's fault that he'd been trained to be eccentric, at least for a horse. His first owner had wanted him to sit on his haunches whenever he heard the word "Walk." He was in show business, for a while, and Blue was part of his act. It wasn't Blue's fault if standing around with his legs crossed at the ankles made him a little lame sometimes. He was trained to do that too. I guess looking casual was part of whatever his first owner wanted him to do. All I knew was that I loved him and he was an excellent jumper as long as you got the signals straight. That is, as long as you got them backwards, which was the same to Blue as getting them straight.

Blue had potential. He had spirit as they say in the horse jumping business. That was good. With a little help and understanding, both of which I was prepared to give, he could be even better. I for one thought he could be great. All he needed was a place to stay, and me.

While the phone at Camp Chucalucup rang and rang, I rehearsed just what I would say to Mr. Hildebrande. Nothing seemed to sound exactly right to me. Then I decided I'd just come right out and explain the entire situation to him logically and calmly. If that didn't work, I was prepared to get hysterical. The phone stopped ringing, and it sounded like someone had finally picked it up. However, all I got was a recorded message of Mr. Hildebrande singing the camp song slowly, to the tune of "Ta, rah, rah, boom te a."

"We're Chucalucup girls,
We're Chucalucup girls,
We are not stuck up girls,
We're Chucalucup girls."

He sang rather well and I recalled that our camp nurse once said he'd been an entertainer a long time ago.

The song was followed by Mr. Hildebrande saying that he'd gone to Florida, and included a phone number in Miami where he could be reached in case of an emergency. This was definitely an emergency, so I wrote the number down and tried to call him there. All I got was a recorded message repeating the camp song in case I hadn't heard it the first time. This was followed by Mr. Hildebrande saying he was driving his way to Florida, and expected to arrive in a few days.

My only alternative was to explain everything to the man who was supposed to call me the next day at my grandmother's to arrange delivery of Blue.

Monday morning found Wil and me eating breakfast alone. Our mother was having her breakfast at a women's club that was supporting her nomination. There was a lot more to running for office than I ever knew existed. She was keeping very busy. There was a bright side to it as far as I was concerned. For one thing, it seemed to take her mind off any problems she was having with my father. If anything, they appeared to be getting along much better since they had a new interest. He was even helping her campaign. He asked all his patients to vote for her, and most of them agreed. It was good to know that they were on her side. Their votes counted just as much as anyone else's.

I spent a very nervous several hours at school waiting for the day to end. That was so I could go to my grandmother's and spend some more nervous time waiting for the man with the van to call. Marcie was almost as nervous about it as I was. Every time I saw her between classes or at lunch, she'd ask, "So what are you going to do?"

My answer was always the same. I wasn't exactly sure. She kept asking though, just in case divine inspiration hit me in the middle of class. She wanted to be the first to know, right after me.

After school, she was waiting for me outside with Tara.

"So what are you going to do?" they both asked at the same time.

"I intend to go to my grandmother's and plead with whoever calls me on the phone."

They agreed that it was the best thing to do under the circumstances. They even wanted to come with me and wait for the call, just to hear me grovel.

"What else are friends for?" Marcie asked brightly.

My stomach was in such a knot that I skipped my usual slice of pizza. Tara and Marcie seemed to have lovely appetites though, and ate as if this was their first after school snack in decades. I sipped my soda and tried to comfort myself with Arthur's last words. All I could think of though was his ears waving at me, and sometimes I almost wanted to cry. Not because of his ears, but because life seemed so simple back when just his doing that could take my mind off all my troubles.

It was something like when you were just a kid and one of your parents kissed a hurt to make it go away. It was always so comforting. Then, as you got a little older, and you realized that it wasn't going to do any good at all as far as the pain was concerned, somehow it almost made things worse.

We sat in the pizza parlor until my friends finally finished stuffing their faces. Not that I could blame them. The pizza is excellent there, but I didn't think Marcie and Tara had to enjoy it as much as they were enjoying it that day. Not that I believed they were doing it on purpose. They always enjoyed hanging out for a while after school, chattering and nibbling all at the same time. So did I, usually. However, in view of the awful circumstances, I would have appreciated a little loss of appetite on everybody's part.

Once, when a favorite singer of Tara's got married, she felt positively sick. She practically went into deep mourning. She carried his neatly folded picture around for days. No matter where we went, she'd take it out of her pocket very carefully, unfold it, and look at it as if he'd died. We all thought she'd never get over it. She almost didn't, until she finally decided she liked another band better anyway, and crumpled him up in the middle of math class.

The point is though, that while she was still temporarily heartbroken, I didn't go around eating pizza after school while she suffered, except maybe to keep my strength up. Even then, though, I at least had the compassion to stop chewing every time she moaned. It was the least I could do. After all, she is one of my best friends.

They finally finished their orgy of cheese and tomato sauce, and we walked to my grandmother's.

"Are you sure you want to come in?" I asked them.

"We wouldn't miss this for the world," Marcie said, while Tara nodded.

"I love your grandmother's house," Tara added. "Can we sit in the garden?"

I got the mail as we went inside. This time there were no letters for me, not even a reminder about the geraniums. There was a phone bill for Grandma, but it seemed too soon for the calls to Mr. Hildebrande and Lily to be on it. They'd probably show up the next time around, after I had the opportunity to tell my grandmother about them. I certainly wished she was there right then. Between her understanding nature and Arthur's influence, I was sure we could get something done for Blue and me.

I put the mail on her writing desk, and we all went to sit in the garden. Marcie wanted to water the plants, because she likes doing things like that. While she did, Tara and I opened one of the umbrellas and took out our books. I did try to study, but for some reason kept finding myself reading the same line and waiting for the phone to ring. Marcie came out of the potting shed and sat with us.

"When is this person supposed to call anyway?" she asked. I think she was afraid she'd have to leave before being a witness to my humiliation. I felt like the person in all the movies who shows up at the warden's office just before an execution to plead for a delay. Marcie opened one of her books, looked at her watch, and sat there reading in time to one of her feet tapping on the brick paving. It seemed to me that hours were passing, but really, we'd just been sitting there for a few minutes before the phone rang.

I got up, knocking my chair over in the process, and rushed into the house. Marcie and Tara followed right behind me. They stood on either side of me while I picked up the receiver and croaked a nervous "Hello?" I cleared my throat. I wanted to be calm and quiet. After all, this person was calling me from the country, where things are calm and quiet. I prepared to calmly and quietly explain the situation.

"Miss Roswell?" A voice shouted at me through the telephone. Maybe he thought he was talking to my grandmother.

"Yes?" I answered, pulling the receiver a few inches away from my ear to avoid total deafness. Even Tara and Marcie could hear him clearly.

"Mr. Hildebrande told me to call you," he shouted.

"Yes?" I said again, starting to sound like a stuck recording.

"It's about this horse," the voice called loudly.

"Yes?" I answered.

"She's a woman of a few words," Marcie said to Tara.

"Try saying no next time," Tara suggested. Marcie giggled and I shushed them both.

"Where do you want me to bring it?" the person asked, sounding a little urgent.

"I wanted to talk to you about that," I said, hesitantly. "You see . . ."

"You'll have to speak up," he yelled. "There's so much noise here."

Maybe, I thought, he's in a noisy part of the country.

"I said, I wanted to talk to you about that," I repeated.

"Can't it wait until I see you?" he asked, just as the sound of a car horn came through my earpiece. "I'm double-parked," he called. "And there's a lot of traffic."

"Maybe you can call me back," I suggested at the top of my lungs. "Or maybe I can call you. What's your number?"

"I'm in a phone booth," he hollered. "It doesn't seem to have a number."

That was surprising. I thought things like that happened only in New York. "Where are you anyway?" I asked. "Maybe I can call you later."

"I'm near the Fifty-ninth Street Bridge," he answered, and we all looked at one another.

That was surprising. It never occurred to me that they'd have a Fifty-ninth Street Bridge in Massachusetts.

"Which Fifty-ninth Street Bridge?" I asked.

"The one on Fifty-ninth Street," he said, a little sarcastically, I thought.

"Does he mean what I think he means?" Tara asked.

"I hope not," Marcie replied.

As for me, I was so busy thinking of what I was

going to tell him that I didn't know what anybody meant.

"I'd like to leave before it gets dark out," he bellowed. "Where do you want me to bring the horse?"

"That's what I wanted to talk to you about," I said.

"I think this is where I came in." Marcie chuckled.

Then, slowly and suddenly, it began to dawn on me. "Excuse me," I said, starting to tremble, "which Fifty-ninth Street Bridge are you talking about?"

"Oh, I'm sorry," he said. "I didn't know there was more than one. I'm on Second Avenue."

"You mean," I asked, as my body went entirely limp, "the Second Avenue here in"—I gulped—"Manhattan? The one in New York?!"

"Bingo!" he shouted. "Where do you want me to bring the horse?"

I don't know whether you've ever been struck dumb. I was, and I can tell you it's a very strange feeling. I do remember my mouth hanging open wider than I ever thought possible. I did try to speak, but the only sound that came out sounded like the one that comes out when you have a popcorn hull stuck in your throat. "Cah, cah, cah."

Marcie looked into my face.

"I don't think she's breathing," she said to Tara.

"That might be best for everybody," Tara answered quickly, and began to fan me with her French book.

85

"Hello," came the voice over the phone. It's still there, I thought. This isn't a dream. There's a man with a horse on Second Avenue, and he wants to bring it in my direction.

Tara stopped fanning me and ran to get a glass of water. First she drank some, then she gave it to me. I just looked at it.

"You're supposed to drink it," she said urgently, and made a motion with her hand as if she were lifting a glass to her lips. I handed the glass back to her. If she wanted water that badly, why'd she hand it to me in the first place?

"Hello?!" the voice shouted again.

"He's still there," Marcie whispered.

"Are you sure?" Tara asked, and looked at the phone.

"HELLOOOO," the voice called, even louder than before.

"I'm sure," Marcie moaned. Then she took the phone from my limp hand, as Tara dipped her fingers into the water and flicked droplets into my face.

"Hello?" Marcie said tentatively. "Did you want to speak to someone?" she asked, her voice very high in her throat.

"Is Miss Roswell there?" he bellowed, sounding a little impatient.

"Uh, she can't come to the phone right now. Can I help you?"

He told her the same thing he told me. He had a horse to deliver and he wanted to get it done. He added, by way of an urgent explanation, that his daughter was having a baby in Rhode Island,

and he had to get going. Besides, he added, he'd heard strange stories about what happens in the city after dark.

By this time, Tara had given up flicking water at me with her fingertips and was now dipping her entire hand into the glass for the benefit of my face. I wasn't sure which I'd do first, choke or drown. It seemed like an awful choice. I felt strangely numb. Maybe, I thought, I'm having a stroke. Maybe if I was, I thought, my parents would feel sorry for me. Maybe I could explain to the man on the phone that I was no longer fit to ride.

The next thing I recall becoming aware of was the sound of the receiver dropping into its cradle as Marcie hung up. No one said anything for a moment or two.

"What, what happened?" I asked her.

"He said, 'fine,'" she answered.

"Fine what?" I asked. Maybe she'd explained my new physical condition, and the voice on the phone was taking Blue to Rhode Island. It could be a present for his new grandchild.

"He said . . ." Marcie hesitated. "Fine, he'll be right over."

"Right over where?" Tara asked.

"Here," Marcie answered. With that, Tara began to flick water into her own face.

"Marcie!" I cried. "You told him to bring Blue here?"

"What else was I supposed to tell him?" she asked.

"You could have told him I passed away suddenly.

You could have told him something," I said, and lay my head on the telephone table.

"I tried to," she said. "But the feeling I got from what he was saying was that he was either going to bring Blue here, or someplace else," she added, and she said the words "someplace else" very ominously.

I raised my head. Tara and I looked at each other.

"Ohhh," we both said at the same time.

# Chapter Nine

The three of us sat near the phone table without speaking for a very long time and waited for the doorbell to ring. Our knees were practically touching, as if we were huddled around a camp fire someplace. Personally, I was waiting to wake up from what I was trying to convince myself was an unwelcome dream.

"What are we going to do?" I finally asked when I gave up on that hope.

Marcie looked at her watch.

"I have to leave soon," she suggested.

"You can't leave now," Tara said. "I have to leave soon, and we can't leave Tiffin all alone."

"Thanks," I said weakly.

"Okay." Marcie sighed. "Neither of us will leave. But I have to call home."

They both used the phone to explain to their parents that they were helping me with something at my grandmother's house. Then we went back to sitting with our knees practically touching.

"What are we going to do?" Tara asked.

"I asked first," I said.

"That's right," Marcie agreed. "I heard her. But what are we going to do?"

"If only my grandmother were here," I moaned. "She'd know what to do."

"We could call my grandmother," Marcie suggested. "But I don't think she'd know what to do. Not in this case anyway. Now if one of us had a sore throat or something, then she'd know what to do. She always does."

"I'll keep that in mind," Tara said, "the next time I have a sore throat. Say, maybe we can tell her Blue has a sore throat."

"I don't think she does horse throats," Marcie said, and we all laughed at her pun. By that time, we would have laughed at an earthquake.

"I'll just have to call my parents and explain," I said, knowing they weren't going to be there when I did. They weren't, and in a way I was hugely relieved. How could I even start? Then it seemed we all got the same idea at the same time. Our heads turned as if they were one, and our eyes settled on the potting shed in my grandmother's brick backyard.

"But what about the neighbors?" Marcie asked breathlessly.

"What about them?" Tara asked.

"They're bound to see us bring him in," I said, thinking of all those windows with people with nothing better to do than watch out for strange horses. "They'll call the police or something."

"We have to get him in without anyone seeing," Marcie said, and began to think how. "Maybe we can walk him in backwards. If anyone sees him, they'll think he's leaving."

"He won't walk in backwards," I moaned. "I just hope he doesn't sit down in the street and cause a traffic jam."

"Say," Tara chirped, "they'd probably put that on television news."

"That's all Tiffin needs," Marcie said. "Her father was on last week jumping up and down, and her horse could be on this week blocking traffic. That would be the end of whatever reputation she has left."

Then the doorbell rang. It sounded louder than I'd ever heard it. We were all startled two inches into the air.

"Wait a minute," I said. "I have an idea. Follow me."

We went out into the garden. I took one of the large umbrellas out of its hole in the table. Tara and Marcie quickly took the other two. We went out into the street carrying them. The man with the van was parked out front. We said hello, and opened the umbrellas.

"What are they for?" the van driver asked.

"Just in case Blue's allergic to sunlight," I said quickly. He just shrugged his shoulders. I suppose he thought that everything he'd ever heard about city folks was true.

"Hi, Blue," I cooed as his head came out of the van. For that moment, I forgot about all the problems involved. I'd saved Blue, for the time being anyway, and here he was. He looked at me and nickered. He recognized me. I'm sure of it.

Wil once told me horses weren't that bright. I think he was being mean. He told me a horse's brain was the size of a small apple. I don't know if that's true or not. What I do know is that as far as heart is concerned, a horse's must be the size of a melon. They're faithful and strong, and willing to try. As for me, I'd rather know someone with a small brain and a big heart, than the other way around. Of course, it's always nice to know someone who has an equal amount of both. It was obvious to me that my horse was one of those creatures.

Blue batted his long silky eyelashes at me once or twice, and I could feel the joy squeezing itself up and down my spine.

"Okay now," Marcie called like a team captain. "All together now." We huddled the umbrellas over Blue as I guided him from the van and onto the sidewalk. We must have looked like one of those amusement park caterpillar rides where the top opens and closes like an awning. No one would be able to see anything at all from above, and from the side all that showed were ten legs marching to Marcie's call. "Everybody, small steps now. Small steps. Left, now right, left, watch out for the fence."

The man who'd driven him in just stood near his van scratching the top of his head in wonder.

"Are you girls taking that horse into that house?" he asked as I opened the downstairs door. It wasn't easy either. I had to hold Blue's lead line between my teeth while I balanced my umbrella in one hand and groped for the doorknob with the other.

"Shhh," Tara whispered loud enough for him to hear. "It's a surprise."

"Well, I'll be." He chuckled and climbed back into his truck.

"And good luck in Rhode Island," Marcie called after him, but I don't know if he heard her. He was too busy shaking his head and smiling. Just wait till he told them this one back home.

Naturally, the open umbrellas wouldn't fit through the door. I folded mine as Blue's head came in. Then Tara folded hers for his middle, and Marcie brought up the rear, if you'll excuse the expression.

Blue looked around inquisitively as we led him through the hallway. This was his first experience with the inside of a house, and I think he was curious to see how people lived. The first swish of his tail toppled grandma's potted palm tree. The second tumbled a lamp. We began to hurry him through the rest of the downstairs floor of the apartment before he did any more damage. I wasn't sure just what he'd eaten that day, and the last thing we needed was an accident on my grandmother's Persian rugs.

Luckily we'd left the door to the garden open. I stuck my head out first and checked to see if we had any onlookers overhead. It seemed to me I could make out the sun glinting off someone's binoculars, so I opened my umbrella again as Blue's head joined me outside. Tara opened hers, and Marcie followed.

"Okay," Marcie called out again. "Small steps, left, right, and quickly."

My heart was pounding as we scurried into the garden and towards the potting shed. Blue looked bewildered when we finally got him inside. I don't think he'd had anything for breakfast at all, because before anyone could stop him, he ate grandma's geraniums.

"Say," Tara asked as I wrestled him for the potted plants, "what have you got here, a horse or a goat?"

"Sometimes I wonder," I answered forlornly as I gazed at the leftover stems.

"You'd better watch out," she warned. "He might eat the building for dessert."

Food hadn't occurred to me at all. What would he eat for the rest of the day? I could always go to the stable, but they might think it unusual for me to ask for a bale of hay. I could say I wanted to make a mattress, but I was unwilling to get into a pattern of lying for the rest of my life. They say one thing leads to another, and I had enough on my hands already.

Marcie volunteered to go to the greengrocer around the corner. She said she'd see what they had that could serve as horse food. There were always carrots, of course. We pooled our money, and I asked her to get lots. Blue would think he'd died and gone to heaven.

While Marcie went on her mission of mercy, I rummaged around Grandma's kitchen and found a basin under the sink. Tara and I filled it with water, and Blue drank it dry. It was very crowded in the potting shed, so I said "Walk" to Blue, and he sat down. Tara was amazed.

"Do all horses do that?" she asked.

"Not as far as I know, Tara. Blue's special."

"I'll say he is," she said, and refilled the basin.

Marcie came back carrying two bulging plastic shopping bags. "I got the carrots," she said, and held up one of the bags.

Blue smelled his favorite snack and got up. Marcie held the bag out to him and he began munching the carrots, tops and all. I said "Walk," again, and Blue settled himself down happily with his treasure.

"Say," Marcie gasped, "that's a talented horse you've got there."

"Thank you." I smiled proudly. It was funny how a habit that looked so strange in the country was an actual asset right here at home. Now that there was some room again in the shed, we sat down on the floor with Blue and happily watched him eat.

"Do you suppose he knows how to play bridge?" Tara asked, admiring Blue's dainty posture. "My parents are always looking for a fourth player."

"He'd never fit in your elevator, Tara. By the way, Marcie," I asked, "what's in that other bag?"

"Bean sprouts," she proclaimed triumphantly. "I bought all they had. The people at the store think I'm a health nut."

"Well they were half right." Tara giggled.

We all laughed. Everything seemed all right

now. I knew I was still deeply in trouble, but at least Blue wasn't, so everything seemed fine anyway. Blue looked positively happy. My friends fell in love with him too. He seemed to sense it. He looked at us one at a time as he munched, and if horses can smile—and I know he can—he smiled at all of us that night.

# Chapter Ten

Wil was autographing his soccer ball when I got home. I suppose he thought he needed the practice. Needless to say, I didn't intend to say a word to him about Blue. It wasn't that I felt he couldn't be trusted; he definitely could. He never said anything about anything I ever told him, unless he thought teasing me about it could be fun. What he does then, when I've told him something I'm not sure my parents are ready to handle, is to make snide singsong references to it in their presence. Something like, "Tiifffinn, confession is good for the so-oull."

The last time he did that, my father asked me what exactly my brother was talking about. I told him that I had to confess that I thought Wil was losing his mind. That quieted Wil down right there, and my father had lunch with him two days in a row, so they could talk man-to-man about his affliction. Wil came home with several pounds of grapes after each of those experiences. It seems my father decided that his problems were dietary, and fresh fruit was the answer. That's probably why he sent us those ruby reds from Texas.

"Hi," Wil said as I came through the door. "What's happening?"

"Nothing," I squeaked, dumping my backpack on the table.

Wil just looked at me. "Come on," he said, "something's up." He's pretty smart sometimes, and sometimes that can be a pain.

"Blue's in Grandma's potting shed," I blurted.

That must have made an impression on him, because he actually put his soccer ball down.

"You know, you're getting to be a very interesting person in your old age," he said with a smile.

I made him promise, on pain of my throwing his soccer equipment right out the window, not to say a word. Not even to sing one of his hints, not even to smile at me in a hinty way in my mother's presence. When my father called to say good night, I stood right near the phone while Wil was on, and listened for even the hint of a hint. There was no point in even bringing the subject up. Knowing Daddy, the first thing he'd do was get hysterical, then he'd probably go right out and buy more fruit.

It was late by the time my mother came home. She gave us each a hug on her way through the kitchen, and said she was exhausted in her exhausted tone of voice.

"Mama," I said just as she was disappearing into her room.

"I know," she said. "Arthur spoke to me about

it. We'll talk it over tomorrow night, right after Grandma's reception for me. The very next day at the latest." Then she went straight to bed.

"But," I said, as the door to her room closed between us. "But . . ." Grandma's reception. The words had sounded like a gong clanging somewhere.

The next morning Mama had another breakfast meeting to attend. It was beginning to seem to me that between all their breakfast meetings in the morning and dinner parties at night, political people must be in terrible danger of gaining weight.

Wil said he wanted to leave with her because he had an early practice. I said it was fine with me because I wanted to stop at my grandmother's on my way to school to water the geraniums. Mama became very interested in that. I think she thought I was dedicated to gardening. Whenever I show any interest in anything, she always discusses the possibility of a career in that field. Sometimes she brings home literature on the subject, including pay ranges and colleges that teach whatever it is I'm showing interest in. I have to be very careful about what catches my attention when she's around.

I left the house right after Mama and Wil did. On the way to my grandmother's, I took the opportunity to stop and buy more carrots. The greengrocer said he didn't have too many, because a girl had bought his entire display the night before.

"That was my friend," I said.

"Good girls," he said enthusiastically. "Carrots are very good for you."

I hurried out of the store with my bag full of carrots and rushed to Blue. All sorts of dark fears filled my mind on my way. What if he'd somehow gotten out? What if he'd whinnied all night and the neighbors heard? What if a burglar came and burgled him? How could I report that to the police? It was a relief when I almost stumbled into the potting shed. Blue was sitting there munching bean sprouts. He seemed very happy to see me. In fact, he just seemed very happy. Who knows, maybe he'd heard all sorts of strange things about the city too, and was glad to see it wasn't all that bad. After all, Mr. Hildebrande never fed him bean spouts.

I refilled his water basin and shoveled some newfound fertilizer into the former abode of the geraniums. Then I hurried to school. With all the rushing around, I was almost gasping for breath by the time I got to my first class.

"I was worried about you," Marcie said. "How's you-know-who."

"He's fine, and he loves your bean sprouts."

"I'm glad," she said, and we both felt warm and close, like good friends with a nice secret. Tara stuck her head into our classroom just before the bell rang. I gave her Biff's thumbs-up signal, although I think it was started by Winston Churchill. She smiled and waved and went to her class.

The day went by very slowly. The three of us

met in the cafeteria at lunch and sat around being nervous together.

"Why don't you telephone the house?" Tara suggested.

"I don't think Blue could hold the phone," I answered, wondering if Tara was getting enough fresh fruit in her diet.

"I don't mean that. I mean, maybe your grand-mother's back."

"I certainly hope not," I moaned, and the rest of the day went by even more slowly as I worried about that possibility.

The last bell of the day finally rang, and the three of us went rushing off in the direction of my horse. It took an emergency like this just to show me what good friends I really had. No one even suggested we stop for pizza.

We reached my grandmother's street, and as we turned the corner, a familiar car came slowly down the street. It was my grandmother's old Packard, and she was behind the wheel. It came to a stop in front of her house, and she got out to help her driver Tim out of the passenger seat. She walked him carefully to the door and then went back to help her maid.

"I think Marcie and I had better keep on going," Tara whispered.

Under the circumstances, I agreed.

"Hi, Grandma," I called cheerfully as she was returning to the car for the luggage. She was very happy to see me, and handed me two suitcases.

"Hello, darling," she said. "How are my gera-niums?"

"Uh, not too well," I croaked loudly, so she could hear me.

"I'm sure you did your best," she said, and patted my arm. "Don't worry about it. I prefer tulips anyway." Tim and the Edna both said hello, and went up to their rooms to lie down awhile. I guess they were tired after the car ride.

Granny and I stayed downstairs, and she put a pot of water on the stove for tea. She opened the sliding glass doors to the garden so we could get some fresh air just as Blue called to us in a soft whinny, but she didn't seem to hear him.

"Well, dear," she said, glancing around for a moment. "It doesn't look as if you had any wild parties while I was away."

"Not exactly," I said, and felt my face turn red. She took two cups out of the pantry, put them on a small tray, and dropped a tea bag in each. "But I do have something I have to talk to you about."

She always makes tea when we have a talk. She poured hot water into the cups and we both stood there watching it change color. She took six tea cookies from a box in the pantry, and placed them on a saucer between the cups. I felt warm and cozy already. I began by saying, "Grandma, there's a horse . . ."

"Forgive me, Tiffin dear," she interrupted, "but not just now." Then she asked me to take the tea tray up to Tim and Edna.

"But, Grandma, I thought we were going to sit and sip and talk to each other. I have something to tell you. I thought that was our tea and cookies."

"Too much to do dear. Too much to do. Later on

we'll have a lovely chat, but take the tray now and please ask them to come downstairs at five," she instructed. "We'll need their help this evening."

I took the tray and followed her instructions. I guess you could say I was being especially good. I always try to be where my grandmother is concerned, but that day I put some extra effort into it.

Tim and Edna were happy to see the tea arrive. They both asked me about school, and Wil, and said I'd grown since the last time I'd seen them. I'm not sure that was accurate. I didn't feel any taller, but older folks like to say it. It really seemed to me that they'd gotten a little shorter, but I didn't say anything about it.

The doorbell rang in the middle of our conversation, so I excused myself and went back downstairs to see who was at the door. My grandmother had gotten there first. It was the caterer. He was delivering several trays of canapés and things like that. No sooner had he put them on the kitchen counter, when the bell rang again, and a man delivered two large tin cans of ice cubes. Another man showed up with two cases of club soda, and Grandma asked him to include some pop for Wil and me. Then a person from the liquor store arrived with a case of white wine.

Grandma certainly knows how to give a party in a good cause. She's very supportive of family members. She even refers people to Daddy, if she thinks they're crazy enough.

A man and a woman from a temporary agency arrived to help with everything, and Grandma set about directing them like a general. She doesn't entertain that much anymore, but when my grandfather was still alive, they had people over lots of times, so she has a lot of experience in matters like that.

The woman busied herself rearranging some of the canapés, while the man carried supplies upstairs to the dining room. The florist arrived with several bunches of cut flowers, and Grandma led him upstairs and told him where to place them several times until she was entirely satisfied. I, meanwhile, looked longingly towards the potting shed, and compulsively tried several of the hors d'oeuvres, but anchovies and cream cheese on crackers were never my favorite snack. I was so nervous, though, that I didn't even realize what I was eating until about the third one. Then I went into the downstairs bathroom and rinsed my mouth. It didn't do much good. On top of everything else, it looked like I was going to taste anchovy for the rest of my life.

Tim and Edna came down from their rooms, and the next thing I knew, everyone was carrying everything they'd just carried upstairs back down. Grandma decided that since it was such a lovely evening, it would be nice to gather in the garden.

"But, but," I stammered, "what if it rains?" Grandma assured me it wouldn't and asked me to please fetch some of the flowers, so I hurried upstairs. I looked down into the garden and there was Blue's tail hanging out of the potting shed window I'd opened just a bit for air.

I grabbed the two biggest vases I could find and

went running down the stairs and into the garden. I stuffed Blue's tail back into the shed through the window and closed it. I arranged my vases in front of it, and went rushing inside for more. Grandma said there was no need to rush, we still had plenty of time before the guests were due to arrive.

"In that case, Grandma," I asked, a little out of breath, "can I talk to you?"

"Of course you can," she said, sounding very much like my mother, which is natural, I suppose. "But it will have to wait till later."

"It's about the potting shed," I said quickly.

"Did it fall down?" she asked, momentarily concerned.

"No, but—"

"That's a relief," she said. "We'll have a nice long talk right after the party." And she went back to directing traffic. I went upstairs and got more flowers.

Nobody ever seemed to want to talk to me when I wanted to talk to them! I thought as I came down. If this sort of thing kept up, I might get some kind of complex. I went out into the garden and put the flowers I was carrying against the side window of the shed. Then I very nonchalantly sauntered to the potting shed and peered in through its door. Blue was still peering back at me. Luckily no one else was looking in our direction, so I turned around and casually leaned against the door to block the view if anybody did.

The doorbell rang, and Mama and Arthur came in. My mother thanked her mother for all the trouble she was going to, and Arthur went straight for the canapés. I guess he likes anchovies, because he stood there munching away, until Grandma reminded him gently that other guests were expected. I suppose she thought Mama already had his vote.

The first official guest to arrive was Bruce, the famous actor who lives upstairs. He comes to all Grandma's parties, and once even had Thanksgiving with us when he was between wives. He said hello to everyone, and then came over to where I was standing guard on Blue's window.

"Hi," he said, and smiled at me in a very peculiar way.

"Hi, Bruce," I said, in my most innocent tone of voice.

He looked over my shoulder, and into Blue's face. "That's the biggest Great Dane I've ever seen," he said, in his most innocent tone of voice. In spite of myself, I laughed, and Bruce did too. "Do they know yet?" he asked.

It was clear that he knew, and probably had for some time too. The day before, when we'd brought Blue to his temporary quarters, I'd been so busy balancing my umbrella and looking up at the neighbors' windows across the way, it just never occurred to me to look up at the tiny balcony on the top floor. It's always a little shocking when someone knows something you think nobody knows.

"Not yet," I gasped.

"It should be quite a surprise," he said casually. "Maybe you can say it followed you home."

"I never thought of that," I said, considering the possibility, and we both laughed again. I couldn't imagine why I was laughing about anything, under the circumstances. But at least his knowing about Blue seemed to make things a little easier, even if it really didn't.

Bruce was very cheerful about it all; that helped too. More guests arrived, and he stood in front of the door with me helping to hide Blue. Once, Blue let out a huge whinny and everybody looked at us. Bruce cleared his throat and announced that he was practicing for a new movie. A woman who obviously found him very attractive came to stand with us and asked him all about his new movie. She wanted to know what it was about, when it would be released, and was there a part in it for her cousin's sister-in-law. He said the project was still in its planning stage, and he wasn't free to talk about it. She asked him to make that "marvelous" sound once more, but he explained that he was saving his voice.

She didn't seem to mind at all. She was happy just to be talking to him. He has that effect on people. At least he was having that effect on everyone at the party. You would think he was the one who wanted to be a judge.

Most of the guests came by one at a time to shake hands and tell him how much they enjoyed his work. One lady even asked him for his telephone number, so they could discuss the arts at leisure. He explained that he really didn't know his number.

"I hardly ever call home," he said seriously,

and added that he'd always been terrible with figures.

Arthur seemed very happy about having a celebrity for the cause. He took my mother by the arm and led her from one person to another so they could meet her too. When Wil arrived, Arthur took the opportunity to snap a photograph of Mama standing between us, one arm around each of our shoulders. Everybody at the party seemed to like that. Bruce very kindly stayed at his post by the door while I had my picture taken for the sake of politics.

Wil didn't stay very long. He took one look at the trays of canapés and clutched his throat. I don't think he's fond of anchovies. It was hard to tell what the other hors d'oeuvres were, but neither of us wanted to take any chances. There wasn't much in the way of soft drinks for us either. The soda man's version of pop for kids was a case of celery tonic.

I did get a bit hungry after a while. I know it's not polite to scrape the contents of one tiny piece of toast onto the contents of another tiny piece of toast, but I did—and ate several empty tiny pieces of toast. My mother noticed what I was doing. Every time I saw her watching me, she shook her head with short rapid strokes. I was concerned for her appearance. I knew what she was trying to say, but anyone else who noticed would think she had some kind of nervous habit. That wouldn't look so good in court if she became a judge. I mean, really, people who have to go on trial are

**108**

probably upset enough without having to face a judge with a tic.

The way I saw it, some lucky guests were getting twice as much on their toast as others, and that's very appealing to some people. I know that several of them studied the trays of appetizers very intently looking for my creations. The only thing that troubled me was that if Mama noticed how popular my canapés were, she'd start bringing home books on catering and then I'd have to convince her I didn't want to pursue it as a career.

The thought did appear to cross her mind. Her eyes lit up with the idea when she overheard one man tell his companion that he was searching for more of "the good ones."

# Chapter Eleven

The party seemed to be going very well, and I
was glad on my mother's behalf. Arthur came to
me and asked if I knew where my father was. He
probably wanted to take his picture. I was about
to tell him I had no idea, when all of a sudden, a
huge potted geranium with arms and legs walked
into the garden. Daddy was hidden behind it,
hugging it to his chest.

He brought it to Grandma, and speaking through
the stems, said it was for her. She didn't look
very happy. In fact, she looked a little sick. At
least it wasn't made of plastic, and the mystery of
why she had them in the first place became clear to
me. I guess somewhere along the line, Daddy had
it in his head that they were her favorite flower,
and brought one whenever he visited.

Grandma smiled feebly, and asked Tim to find
a place for it. Daddy handed Tim the plant, and
Tim's knees quivered. Then my father reached
into his inside jacket pocket, and presented my
mother with a small stack of campaign literature
he'd designed especially for her.

"Every word," he said proudly, "has been carefully selected." It was his contribution to her career, and meant to be "psychologically evoking," he said. I think he saw a whole new world opening for his particular talents. Mama smiled gratefully and took the top one, and Arthur distributed most of the rest to the guests. After each potential supporter had one, Arthur called everyone to attention and began to read the small pamphlet aloud.

It was really very good. It covered my mother's background, education, and career in glowing terms. It was nice to hear that Daddy had so many nice things to say about her. Then we got to the personal part. I suppose my father wanted to appeal to a broad base of voters, because one sentence said that my mother, above all, considered her most glowing achievement to be that of the "average American mother." That would have been very nice, except the printer must have made a mistake, because the first *a* in average was printed as an *o*.

That caught everyone's attention immediately. Daddy looked very quickly at the copy he was holding, and Arthur stopping reading aloud right after the word "overage" came out of his mouth. Mama turned to look at Daddy. She still had a smile on her face, but it was different somehow. I imagined it was something like the smile Caesar must have given Brutus, if he smiled at him at all.

"I should have known," she said between her clenched teeth.

The guests immediately began to read their copies with a lot of interest. They didn't have time to get too far, though, because by then Arthur was hurrying around the garden snatching pamphlets from everybody's hands. The only two people who looked amused were my grandmother and Bruce. Maybe that's why they get along so well; they must share the same sense of humor.

Tim, meanwhile, was still staggering around the garden looking for just the right spot for Grandma's unfavorite flowers. He paused near the edge of the yard, and for a second I thought he was going to throw it over the fence. Maybe he thought the neighbors liked geraniums.

By this time, Arthur was doing his best to prevent Mama from socking Daddy, who was doing his best to back away from impending doom. Arthur calmed them with urgent whispers. Then he pulled them together and took a picture of the happy couple. A woman wearing several gold chains around her neck was standing nearby. She asked the man she was with just who Daddy was.

"I think that's her husband," her friend answered.

"I thought the one with the camera was her husband," she said, sounding a little surprised. "How many husbands does she have anyway?" I could see the lady thinking over Mama's fitness for office. "I should be that overage," she added, and stroked her chains in thought.

I looked at Bruce and blushed. It seemed to me someone should correct the woman's mistaken impression of my mother's married life and advanced years. Before I could say a word, Tim and the plant came lurching our way. It looked as if the plant had a mind of its own and was pulling him along behind.

Bruce stepped forward to help, but before he could, Tim floundered his way past us both, managed to burst into the potting shed, and came face to face with Blue.

"Yaaah!" Tim shouted in a startled sort of way. Then he stumbled backwards into the garden and dropped the flower pot. It made a deep thud as it hit the bricks, and everyone turned to see if a bomb had been thrown by the opposition.

"My plant," Daddy gasped, looking at the slightly bewildered geranium, and probably wondering why he hadn't followed his natural instincts and bought Granny some nice durable plastic roses.

Then Blue stuck his head out the open door, and someone gasped. I think it was Daddy.

Blue paid no attention to the crowd. He thought it was dinner time at last, and was delighted to see his new favorite food.

"My plant!" Daddy said, louder than a gasp, but quieter than a scream. "It's eating my plant!"

"They're a very strange family," the woman who thought Mama had two husbands said to her friend, and took a sip of her wine. "Very strange people," she added quickly, because by this time, she wasn't sure who was related to whom. "Very strange people," she repeated, in case her friend didn't get the point.

"Isn't everybody," her friend responded dryly, and took a sip of his wine too. "I think I'm going to vote for her after all."

I could hardly wait to tell my mother the good news. She was attracting voters, and I had helped. Blue too. She was bound to be grateful. I think she knew I had something to tell her, because she stood across the garden looking very very intently in my direction. She was looking at me more intently than I'd ever seen her looking at me before. Happily, she wasn't quickly shaking her head the way she'd done about the hors d'oeuvres. This time she appeared to be in some kind of a trance. I didn't think that would look good in court either. It's a good thing I was still wearing my jeans, or I would have thought my slip was showing or something. Maybe she thought I should have changed clothes for the occasion. There'd just been no time, what with helping get everything ready for her political debut.

I had a feeling it wasn't my clothes she was staring holes through. It may have been the horse I was holding. I smiled at Mama as best I could, but she just kept looking. She must need glasses, I hoped. She always smiles at me when I smile at her. Maybe she couldn't see me all the way across the garden.

My father, on the other hand, wasn't looking at me at all. He was too busy searching his pockets for his credit card receipt from the florist where he'd gotten the plant. Maybe he thought he could get a refund if the plant got eaten by a horse.

Blue, however, was immediately popular with everyone else. The guests all came over to us to say "nice horsey" and things like that. Grandma came to stand with us after she told Tim to go lie

115

down upstairs. Between having danced all over the yard with the geranium, and meeting Blue by surprise that way, he was all tuckered out.

"Hi, Grandmother," I said, and looked lovingly into her eyes for mercy.

"So that's what you were trying to tell me."

"Well, yes," I answered limply. "I did try."

"The next time you have something to tell me, I'll take time to listen."

Something good was coming of this already. Now if my parents would feel that way after this, we could say things like, "All's well that ends well," to each other, and live happily ever after quoting Shakespeare. Somehow I doubted it, but one out of three wasn't bad so far. If Granny was being so reasonable, I didn't see how they could get too upset. It was, after all, her yard. On the other hand, I was, after all, their child, and Blue was my horse, so I decided to take my time before feeling completely relieved.

Granny turned to Bruce. "And I suppose you knew about this?" she asked, trying unsuccessfully to sound severe.

"Guilty by accident." He smiled. "I was up on my terrace reading a script when I heard him arrive. I thought the cowboys from my last movie were paying a revenge visit."

"You mean the critics, don't you?"

"They were here last week," he said seriously, and picked up his necktie for a second, as if he'd been hung.

"So now I have a horse in my yard," Granny said.

"Every garden needs one," Bruce responded, and they both smiled at each other.

It was interesting to see Bruce and my own granny innocently sort of flirting with each other. Of course, Bruce had to speak loudly enough for Grandma to hear, and that did take a little of the romance out of it. But it was interesting anyway. I thought people stopped doing that when they got older. In this case, I was happy to be wrong. It gave me hope for my advancing years. That was important, because the look my mother was giving me was aging me right before her eyes.

Arthur must have noticed it too, because he went to talk to her quickly and in a low voice. The next thing I knew, she was standing next to my horse, and one at a time, the guests were having their pictures taken with her and Blue while I held his halter. I got to be in every shot, so I couldn't see how Mama could be anything other than grateful.

"Don't tell me," the woman with the gold chains said to her friend and squinted at Blue, "she's married to that one too."

"I think they're just friends," her companion said. "Come on, let's have our picture taken."

Arthur wrote down the guests' names and addresses so he could send them copies of their photographs with "our next judge," as he began to call Mama. Then he called my father over to have his picture taken too. I think he may have been curious just exactly what address Daddy was calling home these days.

Daddy walked slowly across the garden to join

us. He glanced down at the last remains of his potted plant for a moment, and stood silently with his head bowed in respectful tribute to how much his late flowers had cost.

I was going to take that opportunity to comfort him with a reminder about molecules and atoms, and how, according to his own theory, the geranium could even come back as a gerbil. But I wondered how comforting that would be, so I didn't say a word. If I could have told him the geranium would return as cash, he might have been a lot more interested.

Suddenly everybody looked up at the back of the apartment house behind us, where there was a commotion on one of the upper floors. The neighbor who usually keeps an eye on everything must have been hoping for a better view of our party, and he'd opened his window for the occasion. After he glimpsed Blue's head poking from the potting shed, he began to hang half out of the building to focus his binoculars. His wife must have thought he was trying to jump, because she was holding on to his trouser belt, attempting to drag him back inside.

"We'll talk about it!" she shouted to him. Then he spotted a horse through his binoculars.

"Mabel," he bellowed, studying Blue. "I think they're Democrats!"

"This is the most exciting party I've been to in years," the lady with the gold necklaces said to her companion. "I'm going to vote for her too."

# Chapter Twelve

Someone must have called the police. Maybe it was the wife of the person hanging out the window. Maybe he'd done it himself. All I know is that suddenly four policemen were at my grandmother's door, and a TV reporter for a local news program was with them. Edna, the maid, very slowly led them out into the garden. I thought they'd come to catch the man if he fell. He and his wife quieted down when the officers arrived, but now she was hanging out the window too.

The policemen were awfully polite, but they had to give my grandmother a summons for running a stable without a license. The reporter interviewed my mother, and Arthur was thrilled at the prospect of free publicity. Then they all had their pictures taken with Blue and Mama, and Arthur took their names and addresses so he could send them campaign literature. All in all, it was a very nice affair.

The last of the guests left after the police did. They all stopped to say good-bye to Blue and shake Mama's hand. I thought she'd get right to the subject of the unexpected horse, but instead, she sat at one of the tables and began to read Daddy's campaign brochure very carefully. After she'd finished, she thanked Daddy sincerely, and said his intentions were good, even if his spelling wasn't. He smiled for the first time since the geranium incident, and Grandma made him promise not to buy her any more flowers. Bruce helped me put Blue back into the potting shed, and my grandmother called a meeting in her living room to discuss the future.

There were six of us in attendance—my parents, my grandmother, Arthur, Bruce, and yours truly. Edna was supposed to serve coffee, but by that time she was tuckered out, so she just sat down, and Arthur did the honors. That brought the number to seven. I began by saying that it had all been an unavoidable accident. I explained what had happened, and added that I'd tried to speak to everyone about it, but no one had been willing to listen. That argument had appealed to my grandmother, so I mentioned it twice. Granny agreed with me, and that was half the battle, because my mother looked slightly guilty about our lack of communication. Then she said that keeping Blue was still out of the question.

I said that, counting my allowance and my tack cleaning job at the stable, I could pay for half of Blue's board—almost. It wasn't an easy offer to make. Visions of after school pizza with my friends danced in my mind, and I'd have to give up that pleasure for the cause. Grandma recognized how self-sacrificing I was being, and said she'd make up the other half, but Mama stuck to her guns. Arthur suggested we put it up to a vote, and Mama gave him a stony look, so he stopped talking and stared into his coffee. Grandma liked his idea though, and since it was her house, she said we were going to practice the rules of democracy.

Under the rules, Bruce, Arthur, and Edna abstained from voting. Bruce thought it was a family matter. Arthur agreed, but the real reason was that he didn't want to irritate my mother. Edna, who is practically a member of the family, had fallen asleep in her chair. I made one or two loud noises, but she only started to snore. That left the vote in a tie; two in favor, two against. We were deadlocked.

Then Bruce said, if it made any difference to anyone, he could probably get Blue a part in his next movie. "And," he added, "I know someone who produces television commercials, so I'm sure I can find Blue some work in them."

"You mean for money?" my father asked.

"Yes," Bruce said, "and quite a bit of it, too."

"In that case, I want to change my vote," he said, as my mother slowly tore his brochure in half.

Bruce said I'd have to get the owner's permission, and get him to sign a release. I said that would be easy, because Mr. Hildebrande was always saying what a liability a horse like Blue was. In fact, he'd once offered to sell him to me for practically nothing. Mama didn't say anything, but she's a loyal American, and had just lost the election in the fair American way. She nodded her head like a grim good loser, and I ran out back to tell Blue.

I stayed with him for several minutes and hugged his neck while he looked over my shoulder for something to eat. Then I went back into the house and telephoned Mr. Hildebrande at his house in Florida. If he still wasn't there, I was prepared to leave as long a message as his tape could handle. The phone rang and this time he answered in person.

"Hello, Mr. Hildebrande, this is Tiffin. I want to talk to you about Blue!" I said excitedly.

The next sound I heard was his phone dropping to the floor. This was followed by a series of clicks, and the next thing I knew, I was listening to the camp song again. The voice that followed said no one was home, and no one was expected until next year at the earliest, if then. This time though, it didn't sound like a recording at all. It sounded like Mr. Hildebrande trying to sound like a recording.

"Mr. Hildebrande," I shouted over his message, just in case it was him or he had one of those machines that let you listen to who's calling. "It's nothing bad. I just have to speak to you."

There was a short silence, and then a sharp noise that was supposed to sound like a recorder being turned off. It could have been Mr. Hildebrande again, making a funny noise with his tongue against the roof of his mouth. In any case, he tentatively answered his phone.

"Hello?" he said warily, in a voice that didn't

exactly sound like his own. "Who is this?" he asked.

"It's Tiffin Roswell."

"Who did you wish to speak to?" He asked, saying who instead of whom, although he was old enough to know better.

"You, Mr. Hildebrande. It's about Blue, but," I added very quickly, "please don't sing the camp song again."

What followed was the longest sigh I've ever heard. For a moment I thought he'd died on the other end. I wondered who I could call in Miami to go check on the body.

"Tiffin," he said wearily, "you have to understand, the camp is a business. Blue is part of that business, and some times in business, a businessman has to cut his losses. It's just business. That horse has driven me crazy since the very first day." I thought he was going to sob. "I can't deal with him anymore, I have my clam-stand to think of." He was starting to get excited. "I'm not a mean person, you know that, Tiffin, don't you?"

I didn't want to commit myself without thinking about it.

"I'm sure you know that, Tiffin. You know how much I love all my girls, and all my horses."

It sounded like he was having delusions. I was dealing with a man losing his mind long distance. I was almost sorry for the way we'd treated him all summer. I hoped that our hiding his laundry the last day of camp wasn't responsible for pushing him over the edge. One thing I didn't need were guilty feelings for the rest of my life. Maybe Daddy would give him a discount, I thought, and immediately discounted that thought completely.

"In fact," he continued, "I've always felt like more than just the owner of a camp. To my girls, and my horses, I've always felt like, well, a father to you all."

Maybe, I thought, I've dialed the wrong number and was deep in conversation with a complete stranger.

"Yes, Tiffin," he said, in a very sincere tone of voice that made me think he was telling a whopper, "that's just the way I feel. Like a father," he repeated, because I think he liked the way it sounded. "Haven't you felt that way about me?"

"You mean like your father?" I asked.

"No!" he answered, sounding a little irritated that I'd broken his mood. "I mean, don't the girls feel like I feel like a father to them? And to the horses too?"

"I really don't know, Mr. Hildebrande. I never really thought about it much. But I can ask around and let you know." I didn't want to mention that as far as I was concerned, he didn't even feel like a distant cousin. As for Blue's feelings, well, what kind of father sends his child to the glue works?

"You were my last hope, Tiffin, dear," he said, as if he were trying to borrow money. "Blue needs you, I need you, we all need you." I've always heard about how nice it felt to be needed. If I ever needed that feeling, at least I knew whom to call.

"That's what I wanted to talk to you about, Mr. Hildebrande," I said. "Nothing's changed, Mr. Hildebrande. I still want to keep him."

"You do?" he asked, sounding very surprised, but quite normal again.

"Yes," I said. "But I need your permission for something."

"Whatever it is, you've got it. Just don't send him back until next summer, and then, only if you're coming to camp to ride him yourself," he added quickly, starting to get excited again. "I'll even sell him to you," he offered hopefully, quoting me a price that was very low, and about twice as much as he thought Blue was worth.

He seemed amazed that I wanted to keep Blue. I was thrilled at the prospect of owning him. Of course, I told him, I'd have to discuss it with my parents. Why should they object? I thought to myself. Not many people own a self-supporting horse. Then I'd have my very own horse at camp next summer. First, though, we'd have to see how his career in show business went.

I explained the situation to Mr. Hildebrande, and asked him to send me a letter of permission right away. Bruce called it a release. Mr. Hildebrande asked me to repeat the part about the movie and commercials twice.

For a few minutes, there was no sound at all coming from his half of the conversation, then he sang the camp song again. I thought it was his way of celebrating being rid of Blue, so I hung up and told everyone the good news.

I went to sleep happy that night, for the first time since I'd learned of Blue's troubles. Mama was very quiet at breakfast that following morning. She wasn't angry or anything. I believe she was just worn out from shaking hands with everybody in the world. She looked at her watch, and got up from the breakfast table quickly, and went to the television set. The morning local news show was on, hosted by the man who'd come to the party. I wondered if my school friends were watching.

The commentator said something about the "horsey set" candidate, and Mama groaned. I thought it sounded rather nice. They showed a huge picture of her standing next to Blue. It filled up the entire screen. Blue looked happy, Mama uncertain. I guess it was an appealing human interest story, because they ran it on the next program too, and that goes all over the country. Arthur telephoned while it was on to see if Mama was watching. He was overjoyed. He started to talk about running for congress. Mama looked a little pale. She said she wasn't certain she wanted to devote the rest of her life to dining out.

No sooner had she hung up the phone when it rang again. It was Daddy, offering to handle all her campaign literature. She thanked him, and suggested he learn how to spell. They made a date to take a stroll through the park later that afternoon. It appealed to both of them. It wouldn't cost him a cent, and she wanted the exercise.

It was getting late, so Wil and I left, while my mother continued to take calls from people she knew who'd seen her on TV. Biff was in the middle of an intense conversation with Mr. and Mrs. Clyme when we got out of the elevator in the lobby. They stopped talking immediately when they saw us coming. I didn't even care that I knew they'd been talking about us, and that morning I even enjoyed kicking the soccer ball back to Wil as we walked.

Marcie and Tara were waiting for me in front of school when I got there. This time, I didn't even care if people stared at me. One reason was that I was positive my clothes weren't on backwards. Neither Marcie nor Tara had seen my mother on TV, but they were thrilled when I told them all about Blue. I suppose the prospect of knowing somebody in movies and television commercials, even if it's a horse, is pretty exciting.

While we were waiting for the bell to ring, I saw Henry walk into the school yard on his hands as usual. He came over to us.

"Hello, Tiffin," he said.

I looked down into his nose, "Hello, Henry."

"Saw your father on television," he said. "Looked great."

"Thank you, Henry, I'll tell him you said so."

"Okay," he said, "that's great," and climbed the stairs a hand at a time. It's really a wonderful talent he has. If he were my mother's child, she'd probably start researching salaries in the circus.

After school, we stopped for some carrots and then went to my grandmother's house. She gave me a check for Blue's first month's board, and said I could pay her back when Blue started to earn his keep, or I started to earn mine. I mentioned my allowance, but Granny shook her head. She said that every child should have a little pocket money. That meant I wouldn't have to give up afternoon pizza with my friends. That felt especially nice.

We led my horse out of the potting shed, and were happy that we didn't have to hide under umbrellas. At grandma's suggestion, Tara did carry one open umbrella, but this time she carried it upside down, and right behind Blue. It was for the sake of Granny's rugs.

The three of us walked Blue towards Central Park, and in the direction of his new home. On the way, he was very curious about everything, especially the taxis and their horns. At one point, I thought he was going to sit on one's hood when it got too close. He wasn't sure how to react to the buses that went by. I think he believed he was seeing an elephant at last.

"When do you expect Mr. Hildebrande's letter?" Marcie asked me as we entered the park.

We calculated the time it would take for a letter to reach me from Florida. We decided it would take about three days before Bruce could start using his influence.

"But I intend to check my mailbox every day starting today," I said, and we laughed.

I showed Blue the bridle path as we walked through the park. It would be a while before I could ride him there. First he'd have to get used to things. City horses have to have a special kind of training. There's a lot to deal with that country horses never dream of: traffic, crowds, and kids with firecrackers, for instance. There were streets to cross, and traffic lights to stop for, and cars to dodge. It would take time, but I was willing.

Until then, I would ride him every day in the indoor ring, and lead him to the park so he'd get some fresh air and learn where everything was.

We came out of the park as several riders were headed back to the barn, as we sometimes refer to it, even though it's not a barn like the ones in the country, but a huge brick city building. Everyone called hello, and said nice things about Blue. He was happy to see other horses and perked up his ears.

As we turned our last corner and walked up the street, I thought I recognized someone standing in front of the stable. The face looked very familiar, but out of place in that location, so it took a few seconds for it to register on me.

"My baby!" Mr. Hildebrande cried out when he saw Blue. "My own sweet thing!" he crooned, dropping his small overnight case to the sidewalk. "My dumpling!" he called. "My treasure," he practically yodeled. "You were always my favorite."

Then, slowly like the camp song voice on the answering machine, Mr. Hildebrande began to softly sing, "There's No Business Like Show Business". His arms unfolded into the air and, like a glider in flight, he ever so lightly came dancing our way.

"Who is that?!" Tara asked urgently.

Before I could answer, Marcie exclaimed, "I think it's Fred Astaire!"

Blue watched Mr. Hildebrande's performance, first with one eye and then the other. He began to tug gently on the lead line I held from his halter. At first I thought he was startled, but he wasn't. Then Blue began to swish his tail widely, and it seemed to me that he was doing it in time to the music.

He picked up his right front hoof and laid it down gently. Then picked up his left rear hoof and did the same. He swayed like a wave as he switched his front feet, and he did it all over again.

"My gosh," Marcie said, "this horse is dancing!"

When Mr. Hildebrande reached us, Blue kept quietly tapping along. Mr. Hildebrande was amazed too, and he continued dancing as he shook my hand and smiled, all without missing a beat. Blue tugged gently on the line in my hands. I knew what he wanted, so I handed it to Mr. Hildebrande, and they danced gracefully up the street together.

"This is better than Fred Astaire," Marcie said in amazement as even the cab drivers stopped to watch.

"It's better than U-Haul," Tara gulped. "Except Tiffin's father's not here."

Blue and Mr. Hildebrande circled each other slowly. While riders gawked and horses whinnied, they went twice around the ring before smoothly entering the barn. A crowd of passersby peered in through the door, Blue and his partner came to a stop in front of me and bowed carefully. Everyone applauded, and I did too.

Blue nickered to me, and I knew he was hungry, so Tara and Marcie helped me take him to his stall while Mr. Hildebrande sat down in the office to rest, until he remembered his suitcase. Then he got up suddenly and rushed out the door.

Blue seemed content and nodded his head to me after his snack. He yawned as he sat down in his straw and took a nap. All he needed was a pair of glasses and a newspaper, and he'd look like my father in his easy chair. We went to the office just as Mr. Hildebrande was returning. He'd found his suitcase, and everyone was amazed all over again. The barn manager asked him if he and Blue would appear at the annual horse show.

Mr. Hildebrande accepted immediately and asked the manager if he knew of any free rooms. He also said he was going to have business cards made. Then Mr. Hildebrande held out his hand in my direction. "And I have one of my own dear girls to thank for it, and she happens to be one of my favorites," he announced, and looked at me sincerely. "Thank you, Piffin."

"Tiffin," I said, "with a *T*, and Roswell has two *l*'s."

Mr. Hildebrande asked when he could meet Blue's theatrical benefactor. "Blue is what was missing in my act," he said. "A partner I could relate to. Oh, I've had some before; but the one who could sing couldn't dance, and the one who could dance couldn't sing. I had one who could dance and sing, but we didn't get along, and the one I did get along with couldn't sing or dance. So you see," he said, groping for a chair, "Blue and I were made for each other, look! We've already got a booking!" Mr. Hildebrande was going back into show business! I wasn't sure what all this meant for my future with Blue.

Tara and Marcie walked me to my grandmother's

house. They wished me luck as I went inside. I had to promise to call them at home as soon as anything happened or even if it didn't. Grandma was having her living room redecorated and was driving a painter to suicide.

"Are you certain that's the color I ordered?" she asked him suspiciously. He looked relieved when I asked to speak to her in private. She remembered what she'd said about listening to me when I asked her to, so we went downstairs to the kitchen, and I told her what had happened. Grandma made us tea. We sat there and thought awhile as we listened to the music of our spoons stirring in our cups. Then she said everything would be all right.

"Grandma says everything's going to be all right," I repeated to myself, and realized that I'd said it for the second time. Everyone's entitled to a little reassurance, I thought, and said it to myself again.

Grandma asked me to tell her what had happened once more, and I did. "They made a wonderful pair," I admitted. "Just think, all that time they were at the same camp, and they never thought of dancing together."

"I can understand that," Grandma said. "I visited that camp."

She telephoned Bruce, and he came downstairs. I described the performance and he said he'd like to see it. We arranged for a performance the following day at the stable. By that time, Mr. Hildebrande had taken up residence on a cot in Blue's stall. He said if it was good enough for his partner, it was good enough for him. He also said that it was a real money saver, "especially since we're just starting out," he added, creaking one of his leg bones.

I took care of Blue that afternoon and gave him an apple I'd bought on the way from school to the stable. I freshened his straw. Then I borrowed a curry comb and brush from the stable's head groom and shone Blue's coat. I wanted him to look his best, even if his success might mean my losing him to the world of show business. At least he'd have his own income. Not many horses can say that.

That evening there was a full house at the stable. Word had spread about the unusual event, and everyone wanted to see it. Bruce came with Grandma. Mama arrived with Daddy—they'd taken a cab from the office of a marriage counselor they've begun to see. They split the fare; that made them both happy. Marcie and Tara came rushing in just as the performance began.

The dancers bowed to the audience, and then to each other. Mr Hildebrande began a subdued rendition of "Take Me Out to the Ball Game," and tap dancing softly, he and Blue glided around the ring.

Bruce and Grandma loved it but she said there were others to consider.

"Who?" I asked.

"You," she answered.

"I just want to do what ever is best for Blue," I said as I watched him in his magic whirl.

"Well, I want to do what's best for both of you," she answered.

"Let her do what's best for both of you," Marcie whispered quickly.

"I don't want to stand in the way of Blue's success," I said quietly.

"Don't be a jerk," Tara added urgently. "You can stand in his way just a little," but I said I'd rather not. Dad squeezed my shoulder encouragingly, and Mom whispered she was proud of me.

When the performance ended, I introduced Mr. Hildebrande to my grandmother and Bruce. Mr. Hildebrande shook Bruce's hand as if he were pumping water, and said it was a thrill to be in the same stable as a star. Meanwhile, I took Blue to his stall. Marcie and Tara wanted to stay where they were so they could stand next to Bruce. Grandma and Mr. Hildebrande began a nice talk, which Marcie and Tara leaned casually sideways to hear. They talked about the expense of getting an act started, music arrangements, costumes, upkeep, a reasonably priced apartment, and the rigors of full time show business.

"And you're not exactly a spring chicken," Grandma whispered kindly. He did look a little fatigued. "I'd be willing to advance a small sum, to help the arts," she added.

Bruce spoke up and said he was willing to use his influence too.

"Under the right circumstances, of course." Grandma said quickly. She also mentioned having a friend who owns apartment buildings. Then, slowly shaking her head, she asked Mr. Hildebrande if he was considering an exhausting career of travel and out-of-town appearances.

"I was yesterday," he said and stretched his back. "But I was feeling a lot younger then. I think something leisurely might be very nice. Very nice indeed." Then they all shook hands again.

Mr. Hildebrande began trying to sell the clam bar to his brother-in-law the next morning, and a few days later Grandma's friend found him a small apartment near the stable. He bought a lovely sequined jacket for himself with matching leg wraps for Blue, and they rehearse an hour each morning. They should be a big hit at camp next summer.

I have Blue to myself after school and on weekends. We ride in the park in nice weather, that's the most fun of all for us both. It helps him stay limber, and that's very important for his career. He and Mr. Hildebrande have already danced on daytime TV twice, and next week they're doing an oatmeal commercial.

**MEET THE GIRLS FROM CABIN SIX
IN CAMP SUNNYSIDE FRIENDS,
A GREAT NEW CAMELOT SERIES!
THEY'LL BE *YOUR* FRIENDS FOR LIFE!**

Their adventures
begin in June 1989.

Look for

## CAMP SUNNYSIDE FRIENDS #1
## NO BOYS ALLOWED!
75700-1   ($2.50 U.S./$2.95 Canada)
Will the boys at the neighboring camp be asked
to join the all-girl Camp Sunnyside?
Not if the girls in Cabin Six can stop them!

## CAMP SUNNYSIDE FRIENDS #2
## CABIN SIX PLAYS CUPID
75701-X   ($2.50 U.S./$2.95 Canada)
When their favorite counselor breaks up with her
boyfriend, the girls of Cabin Six hatch a daring
plan to save true love!